HOUNDS of PINHALLOW HALL

THE LOST TREASURE

For William
HW

~

STRIPES PUBLISHING
An imprint of the Little Tiger Group
1 Coda Studios
189 Munster Road,
London SW6 6AW

A paperback original
First published in Great Britain in 2017

ISBN: 978-1-84715-662-4

Printed and bound in the UK.

2 4 6 8 10 9 7 5 3 1

The HOUNDS of PENHALLOW HALL

THE LOST TREASURE

HOLLY WEBB

Illustrated by
JASON COCKCROFT

I

A Summer of Secrets

"We could go to the cove and swim," Polly suggested. Rex only gave one paw a vague wave to show he'd heard. He was lying on his back in the sunshine, half asleep, and he didn't look as though he really wanted to do anything, but Polly was restless. There were only three weeks left of the summer holidays and she was starting to feel the days slipping through her fingers. She wanted to have adventures, to explore, not just laze about in the sun. It was hard to explain that to a dog, though. Especially a ghost dog who was so old he didn't actually know how old he was.

Polly gave a huge sigh and then peered round the clump of rose bushes to check that none of the visitors exploring the gardens had heard her.

"I suppose the cove will be packed with people having picnics anyway," she added gloomily. "It's almost lunchtime."

"What's the matter?" She hadn't noticed Rex rolling over. Now he was sitting up, and he poked his long grey muzzle over her shoulder and licked her cheek. "You don't sound happy."

Polly absent-mindedly rubbed away the slobbery patch with one hand. "I don't know. I woke up this morning and remembered it's more than halfway through the holidays, that's all."

Rex didn't say anything and Polly peered round at him. "I mean, I'll have to go to school soon."

"You'll go away?" Rex asked slowly, pulling his head back.

Polly turned to look at him properly. He was drooping – it was the only word. His long wolfhound head hung down between his front paws and his shoulder blades were sticking out of his golden-brown coat. He looked skinny, suddenly, and sad.

"Rex! What is it?" Polly flung her arms round his neck, relieved that he was still warm and there and just a little smelly. The more time Rex and Polly spent together, the more real he seemed to become. Had she imagined that he was fading slightly, around the edges, just then?

"You're leaving."

"No!" Polly hugged Rex tighter and then drew back to look him in the eyes, realizing what she'd said. "No, no, you don't understand. I'll only be going to school in the village." She stared at him worriedly. "You thought I meant boarding school, like William, didn't you?"

Rex nodded. He was still gazing at her anxiously but his ears had pricked up a little.

"William was a Penhallow and rich, that's why his parents sent him away to school. It's what families like that did in the 1900s. There's no way Mum could afford a boarding school. And I wouldn't want to go, anyway, honestly I wouldn't. I'd hate it."

William, the ghost who haunted the nursery floors of Penhallow Hall, had been sent away to school at seven. Polly couldn't imagine leaving home that young. Home, his parents, his beloved dog Magnus. It must have been awful, even though William didn't complain about it.

Polly rubbed Rex's ears and sighed. "But I'll still be gone for most of the day. I probably won't get home until about four."

Rex sat up straighter, his tail thumping slowly on the ground. "But we'll have time after that. And our nights, to explore. And school isn't every day, is it?"

"Not the weekends," Polly agreed. "I'm sorry, Rex. I didn't mean to upset you. I suppose a lot of the children you knew went to boarding school."

"If they went to school at all," Rex said. "So your new school is down in the village?"

"Yes. I've got to go and get all the uniform soon. Mum's going to take me into town."

Polly made a face and Rex blew sympathetically in her ear, making her giggle.

"So. Let's do something. What shall we do, Polly?"

Polly blinked at him – she was feeling so grumpy about school, she'd almost forgotten about being restless. But then a wave of excitement surged through her and she jumped up. "Could we –" she was almost too excited to speak – "could we wake another of the dogs?" She looked hopefully at Rex – there were countless stories and adventures waiting, she was sure.

Rex gazed at her for a moment and then his tail began to swish to and fro. "But who?" he wondered aloud. "There are so many dogs sleeping at Penhallow." He gazed over at the building and looked along the line of windows, his ears twitching thoughtfully. "The portraits in the library or the drawing room would be a good place to start. Or perhaps the carvings on the Grand Staircase. A fair few dogs there. And there's the mosaics in the folly, of course."

"The what?" Polly frowned at him. "Oh, that funny little stone temple thing?" She shook her head. "I don't think we can go there. There's a children's workshop on making your own mosaics, and Mum said it was so popular it's booked out. She was really pleased because it was one of her ideas for new events. She tried to get me to go but I wanted to be with you instead. There'll be people everywhere. Even though no one can see you, they can still hear me talking *to* you. It's hard enough here, with all the visitors looking at the rose beds."

The rose garden was one of Rex's favourite places, since it was just below the terrace steps where his statue stood guard. It was here that

Polly and Rex had first met, soon after she arrived at Penhallow Hall. Unfortunately it was one of the busiest spots in the gardens, too.

Rex wrinkled his nose thoughtfully. "Perhaps you should go to this … workshop? You should be spending time with your mother."

"Well, my mum won't actually be there, she just organized it. She's busy setting up a new exhibition at the moment."

Rex sniffed. "As long as she isn't working too hard."

Polly smiled at him. Things had been better since she'd told her mum she was too caught up in her work. "She never meant to forget about me, you know. It's just that she loves working here so much, and it was helping her block out all the hurt about Dad." She sighed. "It's a pity we can't tell Mum about you. She'd love it, once she got over the shock. It'd be a dream come true, being able to ask someone about the house who was actually there, in the past. Even better than all those old Penhallow family documents she gets so excited about."

Rex got to his feet and started to walk towards the house. "I don't know," he said as Polly joined him. He stared up at the house again. "I don't think she'd believe. She wouldn't see us. You're the only one who can, for some reason. I still don't know why or how. But I'm glad you can. I feel more real than I have in years. It's not just me, either. I can feel the others stirring… If you want to wake another dog, someone who's already waking would be easier, I think. Have you seen any of them?"

Polly chewed her bottom lip. "I don't know for sure – it's like I see something out of the corner of my eye. Especially at night, when I sneak downstairs to meet you. I suppose moonlight's better for seeing…" She stumbled over what to call them. She didn't like to call Rex a ghost, it wasn't the right word for him. He was too real and warm and funny to be a ghost. Ghosts were scary. "Things twitch and shimmer. Sometimes I'm sure the dogs in the portraits wag their tails, just a tiny bit."

"Exactly." Rex looked pleased with himself. "You see, I told you that more of us are waking."

"Yesterday, I thought the china dog in the Red Drawing Room was going to talk to me," Polly said, smiling as she remembered the dog's funny, squashed-up face. The dog was always the first thing she looked at whenever she came into the room and she'd noticed the same thing with visitors. They would smile at the odd little blue figure and reach out to stroke it – and then of course they would remember that it was a valuable antique that they mustn't touch, and tuck their hands in their pockets.

"Could we go and wake him? Or her. It might be a she, I don't know." Then she shook her head and sighed. "There'll be loads of people in the Red Drawing Room. All the beautiful things that one of the Penhallows brought back from China are kept there. And Mum's in there all the time right now, as well. There are a lot of family portraits in that room, all from about the same time. She's trying to find out which of the Penhallows collected all these things for her exhibition. 'Treasures of China', she wants to call it."

Rex put his head on one side. "We couldn't

just borrow the china dog?"

Polly giggled. "Can you imagine what Mum would say if I just wandered in and asked? *It's OK, I'm just borrowing it for a minute…*"

Rex huffed. "Well, maybe not. I'm still not used to all these visitors in my house." He looked irritably at two elderly ladies who were walking past admiring the roses. One of them turned and blinked at Polly, a confused expression flitting over her face. But then she shook her head and walked on.

"She saw you!" Polly whispered in surprise. "Didn't she? Just for a second?"

"No…" Rex ducked his head. "I think she sensed that I was angry. I should be more careful."

Polly shivered. She forgot how eerie Rex could be sometimes – even if she didn't want to call him a ghost, he wasn't a normal dog, nowhere near. Penhallow was full of strange bits of history, history that still walked and talked – and sometimes wagged its tail. So far she'd only met Rex, and Magnus and William.

William's story was terribly sad. He had been killed fighting in Belgium in the First World War, aged only sixteen. He had seen so many frightening things that his ghost had returned to Penhallow, where he'd felt safe and loved, in the form of a child.

From what Rex had told her, though,

Penhallow was full of ghosts – or memories. What if some of them weren't as friendly? But even if they weren't, it didn't stop Polly wanting to find a new dog to wake.

"We're going to have to wait until tonight, aren't we?" she murmured. "The house is just too busy right now. I'll set my alarm for four in the morning. By then it'll be starting to get light but we'll still have plenty of time before the catering people come to open up the house. Come upstairs and have lunch with me," she suggested.

Rex sniffed. "I wish I could. Especially if you're having crisps. They smell so good."

"Sorry!" Polly scratched his ears. "I forgot you don't really eat."

"I'm sure I could if I tried," Rex said thoughtfully. "No… Better not. I'll go back to my statue and have a sleep, if we're exploring tonight. You should, too." He nudged her cheek with his damp nose. "Till tonight!"

After lunch Polly had been planning to have a snooze, too, up in the flat she shared with her mum in one of the little towers. The flat was another of the brilliant things about living at Penhallow. It was completely private but still part of the beautiful old house. Polly loved her oddly shaped bedroom with its round window. But she couldn't sleep. She was just too twitchy with excitement. In the end she gave up and decided to go and look at the Red Drawing Room and the porcelain dog again.

"Hi, Mum!" Polly threaded her way round a family group looking at a beautiful wooden cabinet, coated in shiny red lacquer.

Mum looked up from the notes she was

making and beamed. "Polly! Did you need me for something, love?"

"No, I'm just pottering around. Is this him?" Polly nodded at the solemn, dreamy-looking man in the portrait her mum was making notes on. "The one you were telling me about?"

"Yes, Lawrence Penhallow." Her mum sighed. "Poor man. I think this was painted shortly after he came back from China. It was a bit of a disaster for him, you know. It was a diplomatic mission and it didn't go very well. Relations between Britain and China were very delicate back in the eighteenth century. He loved being there so much, he found it fascinating, but I think he must have missed his family."

Her voice suddenly shook a little and Polly leaned against her comfortingly. It was still hard for either of them to talk about anything that reminded them of Polly's dad. Less than a year had gone by since he had died in a road accident, knocked off his bike by a lorry.

"I bet he did miss them," she agreed in a whisper.

"Mmmm. He had this room redecorated in the Chinese style," her mum explained. "He brought some of the ornaments and furniture back with him. And there's a Chinese garden, did you know?"

Polly blinked at her. "No... I've never seen it! Stephen hasn't told me anything about it, either."

Stephen, the Head Gardener, had told Polly he'd show her the parts of the grounds that were closed to visitors but he was almost as busy as her mum.

"It's one of the bits that still needs restoring. Stephen's itching to get to it, he says it could be really beautiful, and he reckons he can work out the original planting scheme from the drawings Lawrence Penhallow's daughter did – we have her sketchbook, you see." Mum sighed happily. For someone who adored old letters and diaries, Penhallow was the perfect place to work – no one seemed to have thrown anything away, ever. "Lawrence Penhallow had that built, too, to remind him of his travels."

Polly looked at the painting and Lawrence

Penhallow's dark eyes gazed back. "It's as if he's looking through me at something else," she murmured, and she felt her mum's hand tighten on hers.

"I know what you mean," Mum said. "I wonder what he was thinking. Just another mystery." She smiled at Polly. "Sometimes I think this house is full of them."

In the early hours of the morning, as Polly padded down the stairs and into the main part of the house, a dark shape flowed out of the shadows to join her, and a warm wet tongue licked her hand. Polly ran her hand over Rex's ears and then saw that there were two more shapes walking towards her.

"Hey," she whispered to William as they crept along the passage, her torch flickering over the portraits lining the walls. "Are you coming to wake the china dog, too? Did you overhear us talking about it?" She was never sure how much of the time William was around the house. He usually stuck to the old nurseries upstairs but he could appear in other parts of the house, too, and the gardens and the cove. He'd even been up to the flat but only when he was invited. He seemed to like the company, now that he'd got used to Polly. He turned up every few days, even if it wasn't for long.

"I told Magnus," Rex murmured. Magnus, another great wolfhound, slept in the statue on the other side of the steps from Rex.

"Which china dog is it?" William asked. "There's a whole cabinet of Staffordshire spaniels in my grandmother's old sitting room upstairs."

"No, it's a Chinese one. In the Red Drawing Room."

"What, that odd-looking blue monster on the mantelpiece?"

"Shh!" Polly frowned at him.

"It is! Horrible goggle-eyed blue thing."

"Maybe you'd better not come with us," Polly said sternly. "Don't you want to find out about another Penhallow dog? Whoever sleeps in that china figure isn't going to talk to you if you're rude like that." She turned to Rex and Magnus. "Will the dog look like the china one? Your statue's a statue of you, Rex, isn't it?

But Magnus's one isn't him, it's another one exactly like you. They're a pair…"

"Looks like me, though," Magnus said gruffly. "Except the nose is too long."

"Because your nose is positively squashed," Rex muttered. "And yes, Polly, the dog from the china figure will look something like its sleeping place. But not blue. Or at least, I hope not…"

"So it'll be a little dog?" Polly was pretty sure that the china statue was only about thirty centimetres tall, so they were probably talking about something like a dachshund.

Rex heaved a great sigh. "You do ask so many questions. Maybe, maybe not. I expect it'll be a lapdog. One of those fluffy creatures. There have been a good many in the house over the years." He sniffed and, in the moonlight, Polly could see his faintly scornful face. She felt a little sorry for the dog they were about to meet.

2

The Emperor's Bodyguard

Polly flashed her torch through the door and the four of them crept into the Red Drawing Room. It was one of the smallest of the rooms that were on show to visitors and Polly thought that might be why she liked it so much. Now the room was full of shadows, the shiny lacquer cabinets gleaming in the light of the torch.

The blue china dog was sitting on the mantelpiece next to a great clock shaped like a Chinese pagoda. Even Polly had to admit that the dog wasn't exactly beautiful – it had strange, staring eyes that bulged out, and all sorts of whiskers and crests. It had character, though.

She stood in front of the mantelpiece, smiling up at the blue dog and hoping for some sort of sign. A ripple in the smooth turquoise glaze as the torchlight ran over it, or a twitch of the curling, branch-like tail. But there was nothing. The china dog was just an ornament and, at that moment, Polly found it hard to believe it could ever be anything else.

"What are we supposed to do?" she asked the others. She'd never tried to wake one of the dogs on purpose. Polly had woken Rex from his statue without meaning to. Magnus and William had been haunting the house together and she had seen them in the garden – William had been laughing at her.

Polly nibbled her bottom lip. Perhaps they needed some sort of ritual to summon the china dog? Should they have brought candles or some sort of offering? Something to do with China? There was a tea ceremony that was very special, she thought. Or was that Japan?

"I don't know enough," she whispered. "I should have thought about this before."

"Me, too," Rex said. "When you woke me, it just seemed to *work*..."

"China..." Polly frowned and then giggled sadly to herself, remembering Dad's favourite treat – prawn crackers from the Chinese takeaway. Sometimes they'd go and get a bag together when Dad was picking her up from dancing. Dad would spend the walk back to the flat telling her how he was going to eat the whole bag all by himself. She knew that he was joking, of course, but still… When they got in, he'd hold the bag above his head and Polly would jump around, trying to grab it. He always gave in in the end, slumping down on the sofa and sending Polly for a bowl to put them in. Then they'd munch their way through the lot, competing to find the biggest cracker.

Polly swallowed hard and brushed her hand across her eyes. She wasn't sure how authentic Chinese prawn crackers actually were. The fierce, proud-looking Chinese dog might not approve… Rex was nudging up against her, obviously able to tell that she was upset, and

William and Magnus were tactfully examining a display case of Chinese vases.

A sharp, irritable yap made her look back at the mantelpiece. A tiny golden-brown dog was standing there now, glaring at them all.

"Well! At last! Are you going to lift me down?" she asked Polly.

"Oh…" Polly gulped. "I mean, yes. I'm sorry, I didn't see you wake up." How very strange – had she woken the dog from her china home by crying? It did make a strange sort of sense, Polly realized. Rex had woken up because he was worried about her. He had thought that the miserable child stroking his stone statue had needed him.

I hope I don't have to be nearly crying every time I wake up one of the dogs, Polly thought, as she reached out to lift down the golden dog.

"I've been hoping that you'd speak to me for ages," the little dog told Polly. "I saw you days and days ago, racing down the passageway after that great lanky creature there. What took you so long?"

"What did she call me?" Rex asked, sounding genuinely offended, so much so that Polly had to stifle a laugh.

"Beanpole. Clod. Hulking lump." The little dog turned to look at Magnus. "Can you breathe up there, or is the air too thin?" she snapped. Now that she was on the floor, she didn't even come up to where Rex's knees would be, if he had them. Rex and Magnus were staring down at her, clearly not sure how to deal with insults from such a very small dog. William and Polly grinned at each other. For once, the huge wolfhounds looked completely wrong-footed – even though they could probably have squashed the fluffy lapdog with one paw.

"So, you were waiting for us to come and find you?" Polly asked curiously. "You were already awake?" She crouched down to look at the dog better, careful not to flash the torch in her eyes. The dog was tiny, with long, fluffy golden fur and soft ears like a spaniel. Her muzzle was squashed, though, just like her china counterpart and she had huge, liquid-brown eyes, as round and shiny as marbles.

"I was … ready. All of us dogs here are closer to waking than we have ever been," the little dog mused.

Polly nodded. That had to be because Rex was awake and bouncing around the house like an enormous puppy. He was the original Penhallow hound, the dog spirit of the place. Of course he would bring all the others closer to waking.

"I do not like to be kept waiting," the dog told Polly sternly, and Polly tried hard to look apologetic.

"I'm sorry, I didn't realize," she said humbly. "What's your name? I'm Polly. And this is Rex. And that's William and Magnus."

"I am Li-Mei." She cast a proud look at the two larger dogs. "It means Pretty Rose."

Magnus's tail wagged briskly for a moment but he didn't say anything. His own name meant Huge and Rex was the Latin for King – Polly could tell he was holding himself back, too.

"What a delightful name," Rex said, very politely.

"It isn't," Li-Mei snapped. "Sarah's father named me. She wouldn't have called me anything so stupid."

"Sarah? That was your owner?"

Li-Mei nodded. "Miss Sarah Penhallow. Her father, Lawrence Penhallow, brought me here from China as a gift for her. He brought the statues, too." She glanced up at the mantelpiece. "There were two," she explained. "One was … lost."

"My mother told me about Lawrence Penhallow," said Polly. "She works here. She knows a lot about the history of the house. You came here more than two hundred years ago."

"That long?" Li-Mei said curiously. "I've slept for many years, then." She looked up at Rex again. "I remember you. You were in the gardens, sometimes. Even Sarah saw you, every so often, just out of the corner of her eye."

Rex nodded curiously. "A clever young lady, if she could see me."

"She was," Li-Mei said, her plumed tail sagging. "It seems strange to be in this room without her. She was my treasure and I was her loyal guard."

"Guard!" Magnus snorted, lowering his muzzle down to sniff at the smaller dog.

"Yes indeed." Li-Mei straightened up. "Her guard, most certainly. Why, do you think I could not guard her?"

Magnus didn't answer at once, instead he

glanced over at Rex as though he wanted to share the joke.

Rex lowered his head to peer at Li-Mei. "I'm sure you did try your best," he said gently. "Magnus is only trying to say that you are rather … small. Surely it would be difficult for you to do much to protect your mistress. However much you wanted to."

The Chinese dog stared up at the enormous wolfhound fiercely but even though she was so tiny, Polly and William didn't dare think of laughing. There was a great dignity about the little dog, squashed muzzle, fluffy ears and all, and her eyes were dangerous.

"Do you know what I am?" she said at last.

Rex looked puzzled. "What breed of dog you are, do you mean?" he asked. "I'm sorry, no. I am rather old, you see. Back when I was alive, dogs were simply dogs. Large or small.

Hunters or herders. Although a good hunting dog was valuable, of course."

"She's a Pekingese," Magnus put in. "A lapdog. A Chinese breed." Then he shook his ears as he found that Polly and William were staring at him. "What? Your aunt had them, William. Don't you remember? She used to bring them with her when she visited and she went into a great panic about me. I think she was worried I would eat the hairy little things."

"Oh…" William looked embarrassed. "Yes… He doesn't mean you," he added hastily to Li-Mei.

"I am a Pekingese," Li-Mei agreed. "At least, that is what some people call us. It would be better to call me a Sleeve Dog." She suddenly seemed to look even fiercer, and Rex and Magnus nodded, as though they knew what she meant. Polly didn't, though, and she suspected the wolfhounds were just too proud to admit they didn't, either.

"What's a Sleeve Dog?" she asked.

Li-Mei turned to stare at her. "A Sleeve Dog is kept in the sleeve of the Emperor of China, the exalted Son of Heaven, as his last protection against an assassin. If the emperor was under threat, the Sleeve Dog would leap out of his master's sleeve and tear out the throat of his attacker." She said this with great relish and just a hint of disappointment that she had never been called on to do any throat-tearing.

"Oh…" Polly murmured, not quite sure what to say in the face of such ferocity. "And you could do that?"

"Of course," the Pekingese replied, her furry fountain of a tail shivering a little with excitement. Then she glared up at Magnus and Rex again. "With the greatest of pleasure. And that is why I am *not* small, I am exactly the right size. You are too big. Great clumsy lumps. No use at all."

"Now, just hang on…" Magnus began, his voice lowering into a growl. "I might not be able to fit into William's sleeve, but if anyone came threatening him, I would be quite happy to tear out their throat. But only if I had to," he added hurriedly, as William and Polly gave him rather shocked looks. "I wouldn't *enjoy* it."

"I would," the Pekingese put in.

"Some of us are better trained than others,"

Magnus said, rather haughtily.

"I am extremely well-trained – I am trained to be a living, breathing weapon of death and destruction." Li-Mei's eyes bulged even more and William suddenly snorted with laughter.

Everyone turned to stare at him.

"Sorry," William said. "But look. You can't ever have been expected to do any of that at Penhallow as Sarah's pet. And besides, I've just read the label next to your statue and it says you're not a dog at all."

"What?" the little dog hissed. "What is this nonsense?"

"It says that this statue is an eighteenth-century porcelain Fu Dog. 'Although these were often thought to be dogs, in fact they were guardian lions, usually found in pairs at an entrance to a temple.' See? Your statue's really a lion."

Magnus let out a great crowing snort. "She's a pussycat! A fluffy little pussycat!'

"I am not! I am not!" Li-Mei yapped furiously, surging forwards and snapping at Magnus's ankles. "How dare you say such a thing? You ignorant savage, I will have your throat!" she snarled.

Luckily Magnus's thick wiry fur protected him but he quickly backed away from the tiny creature snapping at his paws. "Get that thing off me!" he growled. "William, help! I don't want to fight such a little dog."

"You will!" Li-Mei snarled. "You will fight me! I will have satisfaction, you mangy cur!"

"Shh, shh, stop it," Polly called, trying to catch hold of Li-Mei's elegant blue leather collar. What could she say to pacify the little dog? "He didn't mean it. Please don't hurt him, it isn't fair. He's not a trained weapon like you. It would actually be beneath your honour to fight him, don't you think?"

Li-Mei paused for a moment, panting, and looked up at Polly. "You think so?" she said doubtfully. "I know he's an inferior sort of creature but he is quite large."

"Mmmmpf!" Magnus was trying very hard to protest, but William had his hand around the wolfhound's muzzle.

"It would, definitely. With all your special training and – and generations of special breeding…" Polly looked round at Rex and

William, desperately trying to think of anything else that might calm the little dog.

"It's your duty to preserve your powers for a greater enemy," Rex said in a solemn, deep growl. "He is an unworthy opponent."

"Oh, very well," Li-Mei said. "If he apologizes!"

William let go of Magnus's muzzle and the wolfhound glared at him. "I won't!"

"You have to!" William hissed.

"Sorry, I'm sure," Magnus muttered finally, although he didn't sound it at all. Then he slunk away behind one of the sofas, clearly in a deep sulk.

Li-Mei nodded her head regally in acceptance of the apology. "Sleeve Dogs are the bravest creatures in the world," she said, looking between Rex, William and Polly. "And if my statue is indeed a lion, well then, that is quite suitable, for I believe that lions are brave, too."

"You must have loved Sarah very much," Polly said, and Li-Mei's tail twirled.

"Of course! She was as brave as a lion also. We went on a great many adventures together."

"Really?" Polly couldn't help sounding a little surprised. If Sarah had been a girl in the 1790s, surely she wouldn't have been allowed to go on adventures. Weren't girls back then expected to help look after the house and do embroidery?

"We certainly did," Li-Mei snapped. "Sarah's mama was very strict about Sarah behaving like a young lady, but whenever she was busy, we would slip out. We followed Robert and Nicholas – they were Sarah's two older brothers – riding out across the moors, or heading down to the cove to swim or sail. Sarah could swim just as well as they could but they would hardly ever take her out on the boat. It made her very cross. She wanted to go with them on their night-time sails to help pick up the cargoes and outwit the excisemen."

"The excisemen?" William frowned. "You mean that her brothers were smugglers?"

Li-Mei yawned. "Not smugglers themselves, of course. But their little yacht was large enough to conceal a cargo of brandy from France. Sarah thought they had a false bottom fitted, so there was a hiding place under the decking." She looked at William with her head on one side. "It was for the adventure. They were just boys, helping out their friends from the village…"

"Smuggling was still a crime, though," William said. He looked quite shocked but Polly was fascinated. She didn't know much about smuggling but it sounded so exciting.

Li-Mei nodded. "I suppose," she agreed. "But all the brandy and French wine that Sarah's papa served came from – ah – friends in the village. They were trying to avoid paying the taxes on it to the government, you see. Lawrence Penhallow looked the other way and there would suddenly be a few more bottles in the cellar…" Li-Mei's eyes were sparkling. "Sarah would put on Nicholas's old clothes, since he was only a little bigger than she was, and try to follow her brothers down to the cove.

I went with her. We were so brave, we were not even afraid of the Green Lady, so *that* will show you!" She glared over at the sofa, where Magnus was still sulking.

"The who?" Polly started to say but then Magnus stuck out his head.

"I can hear the locks downstairs," he told them. "Someone's here."

"Oh!" Polly looked at her watch in surprise. "It's six o'clock. That's the catering team coming to start work. I'm sorry, we have to go. Will you talk to us again? Shall I lift you up on to the mantelpiece?"

Li-Mei nodded. "And yes, I have enjoyed our little conversation. You may visit me." Polly lifted her back up and the Pekingese stiffened suddenly. Then there was only the blue china Fu Dog, glaring fiercely out across the room.

3

The Portrait

"I thought it would be good to go and look at the school today," Polly's mum said at breakfast, as she buttered her toast. "Just from the outside, of course. But it might give you a bit of a feel for the place. I'm not on duty this morning, so it seems like a good time to go. We'll have to get you the uniform, too, but we'll need to go into Penbridge for that." She looked at Polly and sighed. "I know you're not looking forward to a new school. I'm sorry I wasn't able to bring you with me when I came for the interview, then you could have gone on a proper visit to the school in term time."

Polly shook her head and stifled a yawn. "It's not your fault. You didn't even know if you'd get the job. I was better off staying with Gran. Don't worry, Mum. It'll be OK." Then she smiled and reached out to grip her mum's hand. "I really hated the last few months at school back in London, with everyone whispering about Dad all the time. It can't be any worse than that, can it?" She stirred her spoon in her cereal, thinking that she hadn't meant that to sound so much like a question.

"Of course not," Mum said firmly. She looked at Polly sideways. "Did you stay up reading last night, by any chance?"

Polly tried not to look guilty. After all, she *hadn't* stayed up late. She'd just got up very, very early. She'd gone back to bed for a bit but not nearly long enough. "No…" she murmured.

Mum smiled but Polly could tell she didn't believe her. "We could go to that nice bakery in the village. Buy ourselves a cake as a treat. Then it'll be as if we're just going past the school on the way." She stood up, picking up the dishes to put in the sink. "Why don't we go now? Then you won't be moping around worrying about it."

Polly swallowed hard. "I guess." Her stomach was already feeling a bit weird, even with just cereal in it.

"Come on then, find your shoes."

As they went out of the side entrance, Polly wished that they were going past the terrace and Rex's statue, so she could pat his stone head for luck. She couldn't explain that to Mum, though.

She and Mum had wandered down to the village a couple of times already. The best thing about Penhallow village was that it was so close to the sea – it was built around a tiny harbour. There were only a couple of shops and a war memorial on a little green in front. The first time Polly had walked past it she'd seen that William's name was there, with seven others from the village who'd also died in the First World War. It had given her a shock to read "William Penhallow" carved in stone.

There was a path across the Penhallow grounds that led directly into the village, along the top of the cliffs. It was beautiful, especially on such a sunny morning, with butterflies looping about, and bees humming in the brambles and gorse bushes. Polly felt the tight, anxious feeling in her chest ease a little as they walked along and laughed as a particularly huge blue butterfly fluttered right in front of Mum's nose.

"He nearly landed on you!"

"I know, I don't think I've ever seen so many. Have you?"

"No…" Polly pointed ahead. "Is this where we go on to the road down into the village?" Polly knew it was, really, but she was feeling nervous again.

Mum nodded. "Yes. We're almost there."

Polly picked a grass seedhead and slowly pulled off the seeds as they carried on walking.

She didn't feel like chatting any more. The school was right at the edge of the village, so they'd get to it first. She peered ahead, noticing a patch of blue showing through the trees lining the side of the road – the sign for the school. Penhallow Primary.

"It looks nice, doesn't it?" Mum said cheerfully, as they stood by the fence, peering through. "The building's so pretty! I wonder how old it is?"

The school did seem ancient compared to Polly's one back in London. It looked more like a church than a school, she thought, built out of grey stone, with arched windows. The painted snakes and ladders and hopscotch grid on the playground looked out of place next to such a traditional building. But there were pots of flowers everywhere and even with no children around, it seemed quite friendly. Not a place to be scared about.

I'm not scared, Polly told herself. *It'll be fine. And when I finish school, I'll come home to Mum and Rex, and William and Magnus.*

She smiled at Mum, trying hard not to look worried. "Can we go and get those cakes now?"

Polly peered round the door of the Red Drawing Room, just to catch a glimpse of Li-Mei's statue. There were so many more questions she wanted to ask her, about Sarah and the boys and what life had been like over two hundred years before.

"Hello…" she mouthed at the china Fu Dog. She was almost sure that the statue's strange, moustache-like whiskers twitched.

"Back already? I thought you were going sunbathing?" Her mum waved at her, from where she was crouched by the lacquer cabinet. Polly guessed that she was checking it for woodworm. "Were you looking for me, love?"

"It was too hot so I came back in. I was just… I like this room. I was just looking." Polly eyed her mum thoughtfully. "I don't suppose you know anything about Sarah Penhallow, do you, Mum? I think she was Lawrence's daughter."

"Not an awful lot," her mum said, standing up. "Where on earth did you hear about her?"

Polly stared back at her, her eyes widening slightly. She hadn't thought of that. "Ummm, one of the guides downstairs said something about her…"

"Oh. Well, she grew up here and then married and went to London. There's the portrait, of course. That's her."

She pointed towards a portrait on the wall, hanging above the glossy red cabinet.

It showed a young girl, her hair drawn up in an elaborate style of puffs and curls, and wearing a pinkish-brown dress. She glared out of the painting under dark, rather frowning eyebrows. Polly thought she looked a lot more interesting than most of the portraits at Penhallow – all the ladies seemed so sweet and well behaved. Sarah looked as though she might be fun.

"Oh!" Polly had been gazing at Sarah's face but now she examined the rest of the painting. Sarah was holding a Pekingese on her lap, one who looked exactly like Li-Mei, golden fur, bulging eyes and all. But peering round Sarah, as though it was sitting on the chair behind her, was another Pekingese – with dark glinting eyes.

"I've got a history of Penhallow Hall up in the flat," Mum said, interrupting her thoughts. "You know, the one that's for sale in the gift shop? Maybe there'll be something about Sarah Penhallow in that."

"Good idea!" Polly hugged her mum goodbye and wandered off, thinking hard. So, there had been two dogs! Where was the other Pekingese? She supposed just because Li-Mei was awake, it didn't mean the other dog had to be as well. Besides, where had it been sleeping? There was only one china dog on the mantelpiece. It was odd that Li-Mei hadn't mentioned another dog at all. Perhaps she'd forgotten, the same way that Rex had forgotten so much about his old life when Polly first woke him. The portrait was easy to see from Li-Mei's spot on the mantelpiece, though…

Polly shook her head impatiently. She could save up all these questions to ask Li-Mei later but they were buzzing around inside her *now* and she wanted to know! Perhaps tonight she and Rex could sneak into the Red Drawing Room after dinner, rather than waiting until Mum had gone to sleep. She would have to go back to the terrace to tell Rex her plan, of course. And then hopefully he'd pass the message on to the others somehow. She was sure they'd be just as excited as she was to hear about the mysterious second dog.

Then she smiled to herself. Perhaps Mum was right and there'd be something about Sarah and her dogs in one of her books. Polly hurried through the house and up the little tower staircase that led to their flat. Then she searched Mum's shelves to find the book she needed – *The History of Penhallow Hall*. It looked a bit heavy and serious, so she flicked to the back. Yes – there was an entry for Sarah Penhallow in the index.

When she turned to the page, though, there was only a photograph of the portrait and the same few details that Mum had told her. There was hardly anything about Sarah, apart from a mention in an account book of silk for her wedding clothes, and there was nothing about Li-Mei and the mystery Pekingese at all.

Polly sighed with disappointment and leafed

on through a few more pages. Most of the book seemed to be about the changes to the house itself and when different bits had been built, which was sort of interesting but not what she needed right now.

She was just about to put it back, when the words *Green Lady* caught her eye. That was what Li-Mei had said – that she wasn't even afraid of the Green Lady. She read down the page…

The Green Lady was a phantom said to haunt the cliffs and the cove at Penhallow. Her story is referred to in several family documents from the late eighteenth to the early nineteenth century. She was always dressed in a green flowing dress and appeared to glow, and some accounts mention her claw-like hands. She never approached any of those who reported seeing her. No one seems sure whose ghost the Green Lady was, although Francis Penhallow does suggest in his letters that she was an ancestor who had tragically drowned in the cove.

A ghost! A real ghost! Polly shivered, half terrified and half delighted. She had seen a ghost before, of course – she saw William almost every day or two. The thing was, when she'd first met William, he was being rude and sniggery and he'd reminded her of a couple of annoying boys from school. Now that she knew him, he was only annoying some of the time, but she definitely wasn't scared of him. A green lady who wandered about glowing spookily was a much more ghostly sort of ghost.

"Ohhh…" Polly groaned in frustration. She felt quite proud of herself, doing all this research, but now it would be even harder to wait until tonight to talk to Li-Mei.

The statue shimmered a little and then the rich gold of Li-Mei's fur swept over the blue glaze.

Polly lifted down the little dog and Li-Mei glanced around at them all, clearly enjoying being the centre of attention.

"We thought we'd go out to the gardens," Polly suggested, glancing at her watch. "The house closes at six tonight, so all the visitors should be gone by now, but the cleaners will be coming soon. Best if we're out of the way."

"Outside!" The Pekingese waved her tail excitedly. "Yes, yes. What time of year is it? Summer? I can smell it. Flowers and tree pollen and mown grass." Her tail sped up.

"It's August," William told her. "It was roasting today."

Polly followed William, Rex, Magnus and Li-Mei down the stairs, watching the difference between the three dogs. The wolfhounds' legs were so long that they probably could have managed the staircase in about three steps

if they'd tried but Li-Mei took the stairs at
a speedy trot, her little paws twinkling. She
was quite a short-furred Pekingese, Polly
realized. That afternoon she had looked up
the breed in her dog book – a show Pekingese
looked like a cross between a mop and some
kind of hairpiece. Their fur could easily trail
on the ground and in one of the photos the
poor dog had its fringe tied back with a bow.
It made sense that Sarah had kept Li-Mei's
coat trimmed short, though, if they went out
adventuring together. With floor-length fur
she'd have been covered in twigs and grass seeds
as soon as she stepped out of the house.

The three dogs dashed out on to the terrace
and Li-Mei bounced down the stone steps –
which had no dog statues on their plinths, of
course, since Rex and Magnus were awake.
Polly thought they looked oddly bare.

Li-Mei twirled about on the grass, yapping and
scuffing at the lawn with her paws, as though
she couldn't decide whether to run or dig or
simply roll on her back and soak up the evening
sun. Magnus and Rex watched her with slightly
superior expressions, as though they would never
behave like that. But Polly remembered that first
trip to the cove with Rex in the moonlight, when
they had raced across the silver sand together,
down to the waterfall, galloping and laughing
and chasing in and out of the waves.

At last Li-Mei sank down on to the grass, her paws stretched out in front of her like a little lion, and lay there panting happily. "I forgot how good it was to run," she admitted. "I think the stiffness of porcelain was in my paws."

Rex nosed at her gently and then stretched himself out beside her. "Cold stone for me. It takes time for the life to rush through us again."

Polly and William sat down on the grass by the dogs and Polly turned to talk to the little Pekingese. "I saw Sarah's portrait, in the Red Drawing Room."

Li-Mei snorted. "That! It's nothing like Sarah – nothing. That foolish painter caught none of the life inside her. She looks like a little simpering miss."

"I thought she looked as though she'd be fun," Polly said.

"She was." Li-Mei sank her head on to her

paws and closed her eyes.

"There was another dog in the portrait, too," Polly went on. "Who was that? Were there two of you that came back from China?"

Li-Mei said nothing. She kept her head down on her paws but Polly saw her stiffen. She had definitely heard.

Polly noticed William scowling at her but ignored him. Why shouldn't she ask about the other dog? It was there in the portrait, after all.

"The dog looked really like you," she went on. "Just a lighter colour… Li-Mei?"

The Pekingese shuffled round so that she wasn't facing Polly and the others any more.

"Stop it!" William whispered, pulling at Polly's sleeve. "Leave her alone! Can't you see she doesn't want to talk about it? It's none of our business who that dog was, anyway."

"Sorry…" Polly whispered. *I only wanted to*

know, she thought, feeling a little hurt. But she shouldn't have badgered Li-Mei. With a tiny shudder, she remembered all the girls at school whispering about her dad behind her back – they'd only wanted to know, too. "I'm really sorry."

Li-Mei got up, still without looking at Polly, and wandered away, sniffing at the plants spilling out of the flower bed. She stopped to watch a fat bumblebee buzzing through the lavender as though it was the most fascinating thing she had ever seen. Then she hurried away up the steps and back into the house.

"I'll go after her," Rex said, scrambling up.

Polly watched miserably as he loped away, and then turned back to William and Magnus, meaning to ask if she really had upset Li-Mei with all her questions.

They weren't there. She was all alone.

4

The Green Lady

"Well, if that's the way they want to be," Polly muttered. But she still couldn't help feeling guilty as she hurried out of the garden, darting down a path that led through a dark shrubbery, round the back of the house and past the stables. It was one of the few parts of the gardens that were out of bounds to visitors, although she could ignore the "Keep Out" signs. Eventually the grounds would be fully restored but Stephen had told Polly it would take years to do it all properly. He was a bit like Mum was with the house,

Polly thought. Always full of plans to make everything just the teensiest bit better.

The path led through the dark laurels to an old and rickety gate, with more scrubby bushes beyond. Polly had never actually gone past the gate – there had always been more exciting places to explore. But right now she felt like ploughing through a damp and brambly bit. She pushed at the gate, feeling it sag against its hinges, and then it opened with a miserable creak. Polly slipped through, wondering what this part of the gardens had been. The rest of the estate was so beautifully managed and once this must have been, too.

"Ow!" Polly caught herself, gasping. She'd nearly fallen right into a patch of nettles. "Ow, ow, ow…" She hopped about a bit and clutched at her foot – there was a spray of nettle stings across her ankle. What had she tripped over? It felt like something stone. Part of a statue perhaps? She crouched down to look, trying to distract herself from the stinging. The stone wasn't part of a statue – not unless it was completely worn away. It seemed to be just a little stone hump. Polly brushed away the long grass and caught her breath. There were letters carved on to the stone – a name.

Sylvie, 1899

It was a grave.

Polly wriggled away from it, shuddering. She couldn't help thinking of bones lying beneath her. She hadn't expected that the Penhallows would be buried back here – and it seemed such a little stone. She would have expected huge marble tombs and carved angels.

Then she saw another little stone and another, and she realized that they were all around her.

With a shaking hand she reached out to clear the names. *Tiny. Socks. Goldie.* It *was* a graveyard – but not for people, Polly realized. She was surrounded by centuries of much-loved dogs. Polly got to her feet and grabbed a loose piece of branch hanging from one of the trees. She used the stick to squash down the knee-high grass, searching for more stones. She was looking for something – although she hadn't admitted to herself what it was.

Polly found it only a few minutes later, under a tree, the stone half fallen over.

Magnus, 1916

The same year that William had died. Polly swallowed hard. She was almost sure that Magnus had known that his dearest friend was gone, so he had gone, too.

She doubted that there would be a grave for Rex – or at least not a marked one, he was just too old. But Li-Mei's stone was probably here somewhere. Polly looked around, wondering where the oldest part of the little plot was. But it was all too sad, in the fading light. She could almost feel it, the people all around her who had come here to bury their beloved pets. She stumbled on, the brambles catching on her shorts, and pushed her way out through an opening in an overgrown hedge. It must have been clipped into a neat shape once but now she had to squeeze her way through. She was still in a part of the garden she had never been to before but this bit had lasted better, as it was mostly paved.

Polly looked around. There was what seemed to be a tiny stream, almost dried up, weaving between huge rocks and overgrown with great clumps of ornamental grasses, their feathery heads nodding in the evening breeze. A clump of what she was pretty sure was bamboo half hid a tiny building with an upturned roof. It looked Chinese, she realized. A pagoda.

"The Chinese Garden," Polly whispered to herself. The one her mum had mentioned. She could see why Stephen was so keen to restore it. When the plants were trimmed back and the stream was flowing again, it would be beautiful. She wondered if Stephen had done a little work on it already – some of the plants looked as though they'd been tidied up a bit.

"What are you doing here?" a sharp voice demanded and Polly flinched.

Li-Mei was sitting on the crumbling wooden deck under the little pagoda, staring at her crossly, and Rex was with her.

Polly heard a faint scuffling behind her, and turned to see William and Magnus emerge from the hedge. "Were you following me?" she asked, confused. "I thought you'd gone."

William shrugged. "We did. But you were upset, it looked like. Didn't want you to go wandering off to the beach for a swim again. Getting yourself into trouble." He smirked at her. "So we came after you."

"Oh." Polly nodded and then mumbled, "Thank you." Even though she wasn't sure she wanted them watching over her, she couldn't be grumpy with William, not after she'd just been looking at Magnus's grave. She sighed and came a little closer to the pagoda. "I'm really sorry," she told Li-Mei, crouching down so she was more on a level with the Pekingese. "I shouldn't have asked about the other dog. It was none of my business. I sort of – forgot that this was real and not a story… Does that make sense?"

Li-Mei's eyes bulged a little more than normal. "No. But I forgive you anyway." She looked sadly around the garden. "I can see

that everything you were asking about must have happened a very long time ago. This was beautiful, once."

"The gardener, Stephen, he really wants to make it all perfect again," Polly told her.

"Would you like that?" William asked, coming to sit beside Rex and Li-Mei. He patted the wooden deck next to him, telling Polly to come and sit, too. The five of them huddled together in the rickety pagoda, looking at the lost garden.

"The wreck of it makes me feel like a ghost."
Li-Mei shuddered. "I did not feel so, in the
house. Ugh. I hate ghosts."

Polly blinked. "Are there a lot of ghosts here?
I was reading a book about Penhallow Hall
and there was a bit about the Green Lady. It
mentioned she might have been a member of
the Penhallow family who drowned. Wasn't
that what you said, that you and Sarah weren't
even afraid of the Green Lady? Was she really
a ghost? Did you see her?"

Li-Mei lifted her head slowly and opened
her eyes. She still looked tragic and Polly
bit her lip – perhaps now wasn't the time for
ghost stories, either. Perhaps she should have
suggested they go down to the cove or walked
through the wildflower meadow. It was starting
to get dark, though, and the shadows were
gathering round the pagoda.

But Li-Mei was staring at her and, surprisingly, she looked a little guilty, too.

"I should not have said that," she admitted. "I was not entirely truthful, when I said that we were not afraid of the Green Lady. You understand, I would not readily confess this – especially not in front of those two –" she glared at Rex and Magnus – "who already think that only great big lanky dogs can be brave. But I thought it over last night, after you left." She looked around her conspiratorially, as though she thought someone might be spying on them from the bracken. "I would not like to tempt fate, you see. If I say that I am not afraid of the Green Lady, well then, what will happen?"

The four of them exchanged confused glances.

"The Green Lady will come, of course! She will appear to me, to see if I was telling the truth!" She shuffled her paws nervously and darted a little glance at Polly. "And I wasn't. Not exactly."

"So you are afraid of her, then?" William put in.

Li-Mei shot him a scornful look. "Of course I am. She's a ghost! You would be, too!"

"Er…" William stared at her.

"We never actually mentioned that you're a ghost," Polly whispered in his ear.

"Isn't it obvious?" William looked down at his hands and faded slightly so that Polly could see the crumbling wood underneath him.

"Don't do that, it's spooky," Polly hissed.

"You're hurting my feelings," said William – but he was smiling.

"You do know that he's a ghost, don't you?" Magnus asked, waving a heavy dark paw at William.

Li-Mei stared at him and then at William.

"Is he? But she is a living child, is she not?"

"Of course I am!" Polly said.

Li-Mei stood up and stalked over to William, staring at him closely. He stayed semi-transparent and she sniffed at him suspiciously. "So you are," she said. "You aren't very good at it, are you? I'm not frightened of you at all."

"I could be frightening if I wanted to be."
William sounded genuinely hurt this time.
"I never wanted to run around shaking chains
and making people scream."

"Hmmmm." Li-Mei walked all round him,
her eyes glittering.

"Aren't you a ghost, anyway?" Polly asked
her. "I mean, you're not alive, you or Magnus
or even Rex." She looked between them
uncomfortably. "I don't want to hurt any of
your feelings. I just wish I understood."

"I am a memory," Li-Mei told her. "I was
special and much-loved and my time here will
never be forgotten. That is what Penhallow
does for its dogs. All of us who have run on
these lawns and splashed in the waves of the
cove. We stay here, forever. And sometimes,
just sometimes, a child will deserve to see us
and we'll play here again."

"I couldn't have put it better myself," Rex told her approvingly. "A very good explanation, Madam Li-Mei."

"I can be a real ghost, too, I reckon," Magnus put in. "From hanging around with him all the time." He glanced over at William, trying to look casual, but Polly could see that he adored the boy. Of course he'd even become a ghost to be closer to his master. "I can do that thinning thing, too, if I really try." He closed his eyes tight and tensed his front paws. "There! Did you see?"

"No." Li-Mei peered at his paws. "No, you're quite definitely all there."

Magnus sniffed. "Oh well. Perhaps it works better in the dark. I bet *I* could be just as frightening at this Green Lady. What does she do, anyway?"

Li-Mei shuddered. "She used to appear

along the cliffs. And sometimes closer to the house, too, even up here on the lawns. She flitted along, wailing – horrible desperate cries, like a tormented soul. They made my fur stand on end."

"How awful," Polly whispered. "What did she look like? The book said that she wore a green dress."

"Oh yes, always the same. A green dress that trailed over the ground – dresses were floor-length anyway in those days, of course, though younger girls might wear shorter ones." She eyed Polly's shorts disapprovingly but obviously decided it would be rude to say anything. "She glowed green as well, though. An eerie light shone out of her. Much, much more frightening than you," she added to William.

"All right." William shrugged.

"Everyone was terrified of the Green Lady, not only Sarah and I. The housekeeper would have hysterics, whenever she was seen."

"Was there any sort of pattern?" William asked curiously. "I mean, did she come on moonlit nights or dark ones? What sort of time?"

Li-Mei stared at him. "I don't know," she said. "Why?"

"I just wondered. I mean, in most ghost stories, the ghosts are there for a reason, aren't they? Something that keeps them anchored to the world." He picked at the wood with his transparent fingers. "For me it was that I couldn't bear it out there in France, with all the mud and the noise and the … the rats. I came back here, where I was safe. And then I just never left."

Polly felt tears welling up inside her. Even though she wasn't sure if he'd like it, she reached out and hugged him – which felt odd, because he still wasn't quite all there.

William coughed and Polly let go of him hurriedly, but he didn't seem to be cross.

"I just wondered if this Green Lady had a story," he said. "It might explain why she came back. If she drowned on a moonlit night or something like that."

Li-Mei nodded thoughtfully. "We only saw her once and it was in the moonlight," she admitted. "That eerie green glow mixing with the silver of the moon. But I know her story anyway. Nicholas told it to us." She saw that she had her audience hanging on her every word and decided she needed to scratch her ears, just to make them wait. "Where was I? Oh, yes. Nicholas explained it all. He enjoyed telling us... He was only a year older than Sarah, you see, and he liked to scare her sometimes, to make himself feel bigger. She was a young lady who came visiting at Penhallow, years and years before. Some sort of cousin, I think. She went hunting for seashells along the beach, looking in the rock pools around the edge of the cove. They'd told her to be careful, to watch out for the tide, but the silly creature wasn't paying attention and she got caught."

Li-Mei looked round at them all, to make sure they were still listening. "The tide crept up behind her, slowly, slowly..." The tiny dog lowered her voice to a whisper. "And still she didn't notice, she didn't see. She didn't realize what was happening until the seawater soaked the trailing hem of her green silk dress. Then, of course, she looked round and saw that she was cut off by the tide."

Polly shivered. She knew the cove so well, she could imagine it. She had scrambled around those rocks, looking into the little pools. She could almost see the lady, tripping over her beautiful green dress as she tried to hurry over the rocks and back to the path. "She must have been so frightened," she whispered.

Li-Mei nodded at Polly approvingly. "Higher and higher, the water rose. So she tried to climb up the rocks at the base of the cliff instead. By now the others at the house had missed her and come to look. They stood on the path, and on the little patch of golden sand above the waterline, calling to her – and she called back. But she couldn't reach them and they couldn't get to her. She made it a little way up the cliff, hauling herself up into a tiny hollow above a ledge that jutted out of the stone wall. The family had sent off to fetch ropes, and one of the sons of the house was all set to lower himself down to rescue her."

"Did he?" Polly gasped. "Did he reach her in time?"

"Of course he didn't! Then she wouldn't be a ghost, would she?" William jeered.

"Do you want me to finish the story or not?" Li-Mei snapped.

"Yes! Shut up, William," Polly hissed. "Please, Li-Mei. What happened?"

"The tide was rising too fast," the little dog said triumphantly. "And she'd injured herself, trying to scramble up on to the next ridge of rock.

Her ankle was broken and she couldn't stand. She had to lie there on the ledge and watch as the sea came closer, and the water soaked further and further up her green dress, until at last, she couldn't pull herself up any higher."

"She drowned?" Rex asked, shuddering. "I never knew this story."

"It's true!" Li-Mei protested. "Robert and Nicholas swore to us that it was."

"It feels true," Polly agreed, wrapping her arms round her chest. She felt cold, as though she could feel the seawater inching up around her.

"Sarah had nightmares about it for weeks afterwards," Li-Mei whispered, creeping closer to Polly, as though she had scared herself with her own story. "Of course, Nicholas told it to us at night, by candlelight, which was much worse."

"Oh! I don't even want to think about it!" Polly whispered. "I didn't know the tide in the cove came in that fast."

"It doesn't…" William frowned. "I mean, you have to be careful, of course, but there's usually plenty of time. I suppose it might have been a freak tide. I don't see how she didn't notice it, though."

"Hmf." Li-Mei climbed into Polly's lap and snuggled up against her. Rex leaned over jealously, resting his muzzle on Polly's shoulder.

"It is a very good story," Li-Mei said, gazing around at the others. "And absolutely true. Sarah and I wouldn't have been taken in by any old nonsense. You just wait... If you don't believe in the Green Lady, she'll come and make you believe!"

5

The New Girl

Mum smiled at Polly encouragingly as she peered at herself in the changing cubicle mirror. "I think it's a nice colour. Much more cheerful than the grey jumper you had at your old school."

Polly stared down at the red sweatshirt. "I feel like a tomato."

"Honestly, Poll, it suits you. Especially now you're so brown – I hadn't realized until now." Mum suddenly hugged her. "We were right to move here, I'm sure we were. You never spent half so much time outside back in London.

You look so much
happier, you know.
Even if you do feel
like a tomato."

Mum looked at
Polly thoughtfully.
"Perhaps I should try
and organize a meet-up
with some of the other
children who'll be at your school. Lots of the
volunteers have got kids or grandchildren. And
I know Mike who works in the tea room has
a daughter about your age. Then you won't
be turning up on the first day not knowing
anybody."

"Mu-uum…" Polly groaned. "You don't have
to organize play dates for me. I'm not five."

"I just thought it might help." Her mum
sighed. "All right, I'll go and pay for these

sweatshirts. While we're here, we'd better get you some new polo shirts," she said, checking the list she'd brought. "But you can wear the same skirts and trousers as before. And a new water bottle – didn't you say you couldn't find your old one? Anything else you need?"

Polly shook her head as she pulled off the red sweatshirt and passed it to her mum. She didn't really hate the colour all that much – it was just that buying the new uniform was making her think about school again and it made it all seem a lot more real. The thought of having to get to know a whole new class was really scary. But that didn't mean she wanted her mum finding her friends for her.

At least I've got friends back at Penhallow, even if they are ghosts! she thought to herself. *And if no one wants to talk to me at school, I can still go home to Rex and the others.*

She pulled back the curtain on the cubicle and scooped up her hoodie, shrugging it on as she walked out – straight into another girl, holding a pile of school uniform in her arms.

"Sorry!" Polly gasped. "I wasn't looking." She grabbed the red sweatshirt that had slid off the girl's pile and tried to balance it on top again. The same red sweatshirt she'd just been trying on, with the Penhallow Primary logo.

"It's OK." The other girl, who had wavy blond hair, the kind that looked as if she spent her whole time on the beach, peered curiously at Polly. "Um, are you with that lady who just went past? She was going to pay for a few of these?" She nodded down at the sweatshirt. "Are you coming to my school? Miss Jennings said at the end of last term that there was a new girl starting."

"Uh, yes," Polly mumbled.

"Where did you live before?" the girl asked.

"In London," Polly said, gazing down at her shoes.

"Wow! You're so lucky! Why are you moving *here*?" The girl grimaced as though she couldn't imagine a worse fate.

Polly swallowed hard. *Because my dad died and we couldn't bear being at home any more* probably wasn't a good answer. "My mum got a job – she works at Penhallow Hall."

"Do you live there, too?" the girl said and Polly nodded.

"Cool! So is that why we haven't seen you round the village?"

"Are you coming, Polly? Oh!" Mum was standing at the door of the changing area, looking delighted. She'd obviously just noticed the other girl's armful of uniform. "Sorry, I didn't mean to stop you two chatting. Do you go to Penhallow Primary?"

The girl nodded, and Polly tried to silently tell her mum to shut up and go away. Mum had that look on her face – *here is a perfect ready-made friend for my daughter. I must not let her go!* "Polly's going to be in Year Six," she rattled on eagerly.

"Um, yes. Me, too."

"Oh, that's wonderful! We were just saying it

would be really nice to meet some of the other children before term starts! Would you like to come over and have tea one day?"

"Mum!" Polly hissed.

"What?"

"Lucy, have you finished trying those on?" The other girl's mum appeared, looking curiously at Polly and her mum.

"Um, no." The blond girl – Lucy – ducked into a cubicle, pulling the curtain across with a sharp rattle of rings. Polly grabbed her mum's arm and pulled her out into the main shop.

"What on earth's the matter?" Mum demanded in a whisper. "She seemed lovely! Why shouldn't we invite her over?"

"I don't know her! I didn't even know her *name* and you were inviting her to tea! It's so embarrassing!" Polly's eyes were stinging with tears and her voice was squeaky. Mum put an arm round her.

"I'm really sorry, Poll. I didn't mean to embarrass you. I just thought she might be a nice friend. You've been so lonely all summer – even before then – ever since… Well. Since Dad died. I hate seeing you wandering around on your own the whole time."

Polly leaned against her shoulder. How could she tell her mum that she wasn't alone at all?

Polly walked down the stone steps of the terrace towards Rex's statue. The night was very dark, with hardly any moon, and her bare feet were cold on the stone steps. She was going somewhere, and she wanted him to wake up and come with her. She wanted company because she was scared on her own, even though she didn't know what it was she was scared of…

Polly placed her hands against Rex's stone sides, her breath coming in quick, frightened gasps. She waited for the stone to soften, to glow with the richness of his golden fur, but nothing happened – the statue was only a statue.

"Rex! Rex! Wake up!" Polly whimpered, and scrabbled at Rex's stone face and ears, trying to get him to listen to her. What was wrong? Perhaps all their adventures together had only been a dream? Polly shook her head. Rex was real – she knew he was. He woke up almost every night and half the days, too. Penhallow was his and she was his person. Why wouldn't he help her?

Polly shivered. The wind must have risen, for why else would she suddenly feel so cold?

"Please, Rex. Where are you?" she whispered. She flung her arms round Rex's neck in one

last desperate hope, but the stone stayed grey
and cold and lifeless. She let go and turned
away, realizing that she was alone.

Except not quite alone. Stalking across the
terrace towards her was a shining figure, tall
and thin, and glowing with a sickly greenish
light. Polly stumbled backwards down the
steps, hardly aware of what she was doing, only
knowing that she must get away.

"No," she whispered, half falling as her feet
skidded on the dew-damp grass. The figure
was getting closer, coming slowly and surely
after Polly.

Polly picked herself up and started to run but
she was so frightened that all the energy and
strength seemed to have dropped out of her.
She had to drag her feet from the ground – it
was as if she was running through syrup.

Painfully slowly, she struggled across the lawn

– she wasn't even sure where she was going.
The Green Lady was supposed to haunt the
cove – she couldn't go there, the figure would
only follow her and then she'd be trapped by
the sea. Polly glanced back over her shoulder.
She was hoping that maybe, miraculously, the
ghost would have disappeared.

But it was there – just behind her! It was
reaching for Polly's face with one glowing,
clawed hand.

Polly screamed and flung herself forwards, desperate to get away from that horrifying grasp. She rolled on the grass, panting and whimpering as something damp and heavy seized hold of her...

"Polly! Polly! Wake up! It's me, wake up."

Polly went on struggling for a moment, the deep growl of the words taking a while to sink in. Then she stopped and opened her eyes just a fraction, dreading that awful shining green light.

She was lying on the stone terrace and standing over her, one heavy grey paw on her chest, was Rex. He was gazing at her anxiously and his dark pink tongue was hanging out a little. He'd licked her face, she realized vaguely. That was why she felt damp... It wasn't some sort of horrible ghostly gunk that the Green Lady had trailed over her.

Polly clambered to her feet, flinging her arm round Rex's neck and using his strength to pull against.

"Where is she?" she whispered, her voice shaking. "Did you scare her away? Where did she go?"

"Who?" Rex stared at her. "There was no one else here, Polly. You were asleep."

"I wasn't…" Polly said, but suddenly she felt doubtful. It had seemed so real. She had been so terribly frightened. Could it have all been some awful nightmare? She twisted her fingers in Rex's rough fur, feeling the warmth and strength of him under her hands. She had been sleepwalking, she realized now, slowly coming to herself. She must have been. She didn't remember coming downstairs from the flat at all. The encounter with the Green Lady had started when she was on the terrace – it had started with trying to wake Rex.

"Why didn't you wake up?" she asked, shivering as she remembered the cold lifelessness of his statue.

"I did!" he said indignantly. "Here I am, awake!"

"No, I mean before. I called and called, Rex. I must have scratched my hands trying to wake you, I – I even hit you!" Polly tried to look at her hands but the moonless night was too dark.

"I woke up as you passed me on the steps." Rex nuzzled her ear with his chilly nose and Polly shivered. "You didn't touch me. You were dreaming, that's all. I think we should go inside. Back up to your room and get you warm again."

"Yes…" Polly whispered. She hadn't walked in her sleep for what – three weeks? She had even thought that perhaps she'd grown out of it. Obviously not.

Rex led her back inside the house, her hand still clutching his fur. Polly remembered to lock the doors again behind her but the keys slipped and fumbled in her cold fingers and she nearly fell as Rex half-dragged her up the stairs.

They crept quietly through the flat and into Polly's room. She could hear her mother's sleepy breathing in the room next door – they hadn't disturbed her. Rex nudged her over to the bed and pulled up the duvet around her with his teeth. Then he sat down – so tall that he was still on a level with her face.

"It was just a dream?" Polly whispered again. "It didn't feel like one."

"Just a dream," Rex assured her as he clambered carefully on to the bed. "And even if it wasn't, Polly, I am here. There's nothing to be scared of." He snorted a little dog-laugh. "Except for me. Go to sleep, dearest Polly."

Rex lay down next to her in the same pose as his statue, front paws stretched out. Polly could feel his warmth as she snuggled up next to him, her arm round his shoulders. Rex lowered his head down on to his paws, so that his whiskery muzzle prickled her cheek, and soon Polly felt his breathing slow, a gentle in and out that meant he was asleep.

But it was a long time before she dared to let herself sleep, too.

6

The Girl in the Portrait

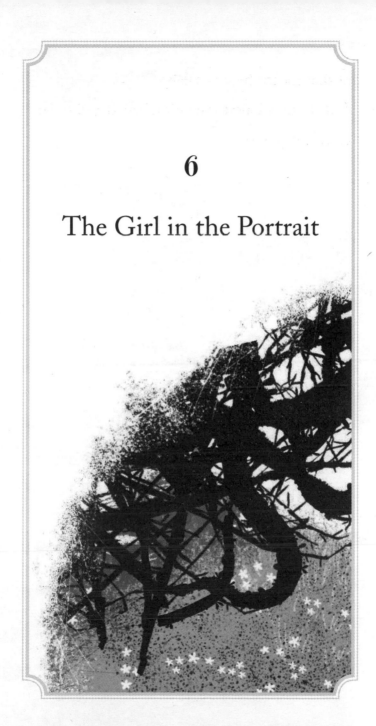

The next morning, Polly was woken by a thorough lick of her cheek. She groaned and wiped her face with her hand. "Ugh!" she spluttered. "Oh…" She sat up, hugging her knees tightly as she remembered why Rex was stretched out next to her. She peered anxiously around the room, looking for that greenish glow, but there was nothing – only the bright sunlight breaking through the gap in her curtains.

"Yes. Now that it's daylight and you're properly awake, what happened?" Rex asked, in a growly whisper. "Did you dream of that Green Lady? I shall lock Li-Mei away in the Red Drawing Room, stupid creature. She should never have told you that story."

"She didn't make the ghost appear," Polly said wearily. "I did, I suppose, because I wasn't scared. Li-Mei was right, that was tempting fate."

"No, no, no." Rex shook his head, his ears flapping. "I tell you, Polly, there was no ghost. Just you. You were fighting with yourself. And then with me."

"Did I hurt you?" Polly asked guiltily.

"No!" Rex snorted, as though the very idea was funny.

"I did see it. I'm sure it wasn't just a dream, Rex, it felt real. Maybe it only came for me and that's why you couldn't see it?" Polly shuddered. It would probably come back for her again.

Rex growled, long and low. "Don't say that!" he whispered. "Polly, I promise you, there was no ghost there with us last night. I would have known. I am a ghost of a kind, I would be able to tell. I can feel all the spirits that roam Penhallow. You know that." He sank his head down on the bed next to her and Polly ran his ears through her hands, over and over.

"So … it had to be a dream?" Polly wasn't sure if she could believe it. She *wanted* to – but it felt too easy.

"You were walking in your sleep," Rex suggested. "Were you unhappy about something? Could that have set off the sleepwalking and the dream? And Li-Mei's story was there in your head."

"There is something…" said Polly. "We went to Penbridge yesterday to buy my uniform – for my new school. Term starts in a couple of weeks. I'm scared, Rex. What if no one talks to me? Or … or they want to talk too much? There was a girl there at the uniform shop and she was asking me why we'd moved here. I didn't want to tell her about my dad dying but the school knows. I bet everyone's going to know about it sooner or later," Polly gabbled. "I mean, someone's going to ask me if I have a dad, aren't they? I spent all afternoon worrying about it."

Rex nudged her with his cold nose. "Why didn't you say anything? I probably wouldn't have been any help but at least you wouldn't have been worrying about it on your own." He sighed. "Well, I can see why you were upset enough to sleepwalk." He slumped down with a sigh and neither of them said anything for a while. Polly just kept stroking his ears, until Rex lifted his head and stared at her.

"Polly. Do you really think there was a Green Lady? I would have known, I'm sure of it. When Li-Mei told that story, all the way through I was thinking, *I don't remember this…* I assumed it was just that I'd forgotten. But perhaps the story was *never* true!"

"Why would Robert and Nicholas make it up? Just to scare their little sister? That's horrible."

Rex shook his head. "No. Remember what Li-Mei said? Sarah's brothers were smugglers – or playing at smuggling, at least. They needed to be able to move the cargoes of liquor and tobacco around with no one seeing them."

"And no one would dare go out on the cliff or down to the cove if they thought there was a ghost! You mean, they created the ghost to keep everybody indoors at night. That's actually really clever! So sneaky!"

"And it would explain why I've never sensed this Green Lady." Rex looked up at her. "Truly, Polly. She never existed."

"Maybe you're right... But that still doesn't explain what Li-Mei and Sarah saw that time," Polly said and let out a sigh. "Oh, Rex. What *are* we going to say to Li-Mei?"

"What do you mean, there was no ghost?" Li-Mei glared at Rex and Polly. They had hurried up to the Red Drawing Room to talk to her, as soon as the house had closed for the day. They'd decided not to mention anything to William and Magnus – it was probably best that they spoke to Li-Mei about this on their own.

The Pekingese was quivering with indignation – Polly could just imagine her inside an emperor's sleeve, readying herself to pounce. "Of course there was. Do you think we just made up the Green Lady?"

Rex lowered his head to stare into her eyes. "We don't think *you* made her up," he said pointedly. "But we suspect someone did – a long time ago."

Li-Mei's fluffy eyebrows lowered over her bulging eyes. "What?"

"We just wondered if you or Sarah ever saw the Green Lady up close? So that you were absolutely sure she was a ghost?" Polly asked, trying to keep her voice as soothing as possible.

"Of course she was a ghost! She was green! She glowed in the dark!"

Polly nodded. "We're not saying that we don't believe you," she assured the furious little dog. "It's just… How close did you ever actually get?"

"I suppose … the length of the garden below the terrace?" Li-Mei mused. "You wouldn't have wanted to get any closer," she added rather grumpily. "And Robert and Nicholas saw her much closer than that. She almost touched Nicholas, with her horrible claw-like hand. They were terrified. They told us so and they were never afraid of anything so she must have been truly dreadful."

Rex and Polly nodded and exchanged a look. Then Rex gave a deep sigh that seemed to come from the very end of his tail. "The thing is," he said gently, "you told us that Sarah's brothers were smugglers. They landed their cargoes down in the cove, didn't they?"

Li-Mei shook her ears. "We never knew for sure."

"Exactly. Because you were scared of the ghost and you kept away from the cove at night-time. Just as everyone else did." Rex eyed her rather cautiously. "Just as Sarah's brothers wanted."

Li-Mei stood up, the fur around her neck rising up in an angry ruff so she looked much bigger all of a sudden. "They *lied* to her?" she growled, low in her throat. "It was all a trick, to stop her bothering them? Because they didn't want a girl caught up in their criminal, scurvy, piratical plans? Rrrrr!" The little Pekingese broke into a storm of furious yapping.

"Is she angry with us?" Polly whispered to Rex.

"No, I think she's just generally angry," Rex
murmured, watching as Li-Mei stomped up
and down the sofa. For such a small dog, she
could make an impressive amount of noise.
She marched from end to end of the sofa a few
more times, then at last she slumped down in
the middle, panting.

"They lied," she growled bitterly. "I suppose
I shouldn't be angry, it's so long ago. But I am,
I am..."

"They were probably only doing it to keep
Sarah safe," Polly pointed out.

"Perhaps." But the eyes Li-Mei turned to
Polly were hard and unforgiving. "They would

have enjoyed fooling their little sister. That's why I'm so angry. They would have laughed at her secretly. Oh, I could bite them." She growled, showing her teeth. "They made up that story to be unkind to Sarah."

Rex wrinkled his muzzle. "But Sarah wasn't the only one her brothers told the story to, was she? They were trying to keep people away from the cove. It wasn't just about your mistress."

Li-Mei gazed up at him and then she looked over Rex's shoulder at the portrait of Sarah. The dog's eyes shone even brighter than usual. "It was her prettiest dress," she murmured. "She loved it, her green silk dress. It was a present from her mama. Her first really grown-up dress and she adored it." Li-Mei shook her head miserably. "She would never wear it, after Nicholas told her that awful story. She said that every time she put it on, she could feel the seawater creeping up the silk and weighing down her skirts. In the end her mama had it dyed and it was a horrible dusty pinkish-brown colour, instead of that gorgeous green. It's that dress she's wearing in the portrait." She looked up at Polly. "You must see what I mean."

Polly nodded, looking at the painting. She had thought before that it was rather a dreary colour to wear to be painted in.

Li-Mei moaned. "That they could be so cruel to my darling girl. To spoil her happiness in that perfect dress. And … and…"

"What is it?" Polly asked worriedly.

The little dog had hunched her shoulders and her head was hanging. As Polly watched, a great shudder seemed to run through her, and then she lifted her head again and howled. The sound was heartbreakingly sad and yet eerie at the same time. Polly felt the hair stand up on the back of her neck as Li-Mei howled again, over and over, her muzzle raised to the ceiling. Then she sank down on the sofa and stretched out on her side, her eyes closed and her little chest heaving. She was muttering something, and both Polly and Rex leaned down to listen, but the words were unfamiliar – Polly couldn't even catch them.

"I think she must be speaking Chinese," Rex whispered.

"Li-Mei, what is it?" Polly said. "Please tell us. Can't we help you?"

The golden Pekingese gave a soft whine and then opened her eyes, gazing up dolefully at Polly. "No one can help me. It's too long ago."

"Tell us," Polly pleaded. "Perhaps we can. You don't know. Everything is strange at Penhallow. You, Rex, Magnus and William. You're all from the past. So it's as though history is still here – do you see what I mean? History is still happening. Maybe we can make things a little better. Oh, please don't be so sad."

Li-Mei dragged herself up so that she was sitting and licked Polly's hand, just a tiny dab with her little pink tongue. "You are a very sweet girl to worry about me," she said. "You remind me of my Sarah." She glanced quickly at Rex. "So I will tell you." She was silent for a moment, obviously finding it hard to begin. Then she shook her head. "No. I cannot tell. I will show, instead. Look at the painting, Polly. You will understand. You will see."

Sarah's neck ached and she tried to roll it, stretching the muscles in her shoulders subtly so that the painter wouldn't see and complain to her mother about her fidgeting again. Monsieur Fantin had already told Lady Penhallow that she was sulky and difficult, and her badly behaved dogs were making it impossible for him to work. Mama had told her off and threatened to confine her to her room, if she couldn't be good. Han was wriggling again. He was supposed to be lying at her feet, while Li-Mei sat on her lap, but he wouldn't do it. He kept sneaking away, and he had already stolen one of the painter's brushes and chewed it to splinters.

"Down," she hissed, under her breath. "Down, Han!" But the mischievous little dog only twitched his tiny ears. She knew he had heard…

"Sit still, please, Miss Penhallow!"

She flinched and straightened her shoulders, trying to remember exactly how she had been sitting. She hated this portrait already, she decided. It was bad enough that she had to wear this horrible dress. She wished Mama had let her give it away to one of her little cousins. But the dress had been so expensive, Mama had refused to do anything more than dye it. Mama was not someone who believed in ghosts. She thought the whole story of the Green Lady was nonsense.

She eyed the pinkish-brown of her dress sadly. It had been so beautiful when it was green. Now it was just a dismal, nothingy colour – and it was still green underneath… Sarah tried to think of something else.

Tonight, she told herself firmly. *Tonight the moon will be full and I'll follow my brothers down to the cove, Green Lady or no Green Lady…*

And then Polly was herself again. "What was that?" she gasped, looking down at her yellow shorts. "What did you do? I was there! I saw him – the other dog, Han, and you, too! It was as though I was Sarah. Li-Mei, that was really freaky."

"I do not know what this word means." Li-Mei sniffed haughtily. "I showed you. You were looking at the painting, you wanted to see!" Then she laid a paw on Polly's knee. "This way I don't have to tell. It's easier. Do you want the rest?"

Polly swallowed. "Yes. I suppose…"

"Think about Penhallow Hall on a moonlit

night," Li-Mei murmured.

Rex leaned closer, looking between them uncertainly. "Polly…"

"I'll tell you in a minute," Polly promised him. "I'm ready, Li-Mei."

Sarah was opening the side door – the same side door she used to sneak out and meet Rex, something whispered in the back of Polly's mind. The boys couldn't be that far ahead of her, could they? She had scrambled out of bed and dressed as quickly as she could, when she heard the footsteps along the corridor. Yes, and there were the footprints in the dew. "Come on, Han. Come, Li-Mei," she whispered.

Li-Mei whined and she crouched down to pat her. "Don't be frightened. No one's seen the Green Lady in weeks. Perhaps she's gone. Come on, we don't want to lose Robert and Nicholas."

She followed the prints across the grass and started along the path through the wood, the dogs sniffing and pattering around her, their tails whisking. But then they stopped dead, the pair of them, and she saw the light change. A sickly greenish glow shone through the branches and everything in the wood fell silent. She could hear her own breathing, and nothing else. Not even footsteps. And there should be footsteps – since someone was coming.

She was frozen – too frightened to run back to the house or down to the cove, too frightened even to think. She could feel the Green Lady approaching, like a coldness settling over her, down to her bones. The dogs were pressed against her ankles, trembling.

"Wake up!"

Polly jumped, clutching her hand against her chest. "Did you bite me?" she asked, looking at Rex in surprise.

"Scratched you." He hung his head. "I'm sorry, Polly. I couldn't bear to see you like that. Your eyes rolled back. I was frightened, just watching you."

"It's all right. I'm glad you did." She looked at Li-Mei. "You really saw her? The Green Lady?"

"Yes. A greenish form, quite small – she was

only young, remember. Drifting through the woods towards us, reaching out. As though she wanted us to help her… But she would have sucked the life right out of us, to bring herself back." Li-Mei looked up at Polly. "Now you tell me that she wasn't real, and I think you may be right. But for the life of me, that night I would have sworn she was a spirit. You felt how scared Sarah was, just then. How could she have frightened us so much, if she were not real?"

"Because you'd already heard her story," Rex said grimly. "Cleverly shaped to fit. I wonder what other stories the boys told about that ghost around the village. Twisting the tale to scare everyone safely inside and out of the way."

"What did you do?" Polly asked. She would have run, she was almost sure.

"Sarah snatched me up and darted away

towards the house. She tried to grab my brother Han, too, but he wouldn't let her. He stayed on the path, growling and growling at the spirit as it came closer. In the end Sarah left him and we ran." Li-Mei drooped again. "We left him there and that was the last we ever saw of him."

"What?" Polly squeaked. "What do you mean? Did the ghost grab him? I mean…" She frowned, shaking her head. For a moment she had forgotten that there was no ghost. "What happened?"

"I do not know," Li-Mei said quietly. "We called to him from the lawn but he didn't come. We were so scared, for him and for the boys." She growled. "The boys! We were worrying about them, when the ghost was probably just one of them or their tearaway friends all along. When Sarah saw her brothers the next morning, she was so relieved. She told them about following them and seeing the ghost. They swore they'd only gone down to the cove for a moonlight swim and that they'd not seen the ghost at all. Robert even told her that perhaps the Green Lady had appeared to her because they were not so different in age."

"And I bet that scared her even more," Polly said furiously. "Do you know, Li-Mei, I'm starting to dislike those boys just as much as you do. But I still don't understand what happened to Han."

"We searched for Han for days," Li-Mei whispered faintly. "Along the cliff. Through the woods. The village boys set rabbit snares sometimes, Sarah was always telling us to keep to the paths and calling us back when we ran through the bracken. She was terrified that we would find him caught in one. But we never found any sign of him at all. Either the Green Lady took him, we thought, or he had run into the sea to escape from her and drowned."

"I suppose that is possible," Rex agreed shakily. "But then why did his memory never come back to Penhallow, like all the other dogs? He was loved and wanted and missed…"

Li-Mei whined and pressed her head against the cushions to shut out his words.

Polly reached out and ran her hand over the smooth golden fur on the Pekingese's domed head. "We'll find out," she promised. "Somehow we will. Come on!"

7

The Crack in the Rock

After Li-Mei's strange storytelling, the woods looked different as they set out across the lawn from the terrace. The trees seemed to loom over them in the gathering darkness, tall and menacing, even in the light from Polly's torch. She wound her fingers tightly in Rex's neck fur and walked close by, feeling the great furry warmth of him beside her.

"It was only a tale," he murmured to her and she laughed, a little ashamed that he'd noticed.

"It was a very good one, though," Polly

whispered back.

Li-Mei, who was walking on Polly's other side, snorted a little. "You should have heard Nicholas tell it. Your blood would have run cold." Then she shied sideways with a yelp as something skittered across the path in front of them.

"I think it was just a wood mouse," Polly said, trying to pretend that her heart wasn't thumping, too.

"Stop being so jittery, the pair of you." Rex nudged Polly's elbow with his nose. "How many times? There's no ghost."

"It feels like there might be one," Polly muttered. "It's so dark and quiet out here."

Rex growled irritably. "And if Li-Mei had told you a story about fairies, you'd be seeing those fluttering in the trees, wouldn't you! Let's just get down to the beach."

Polly sighed. She could tell that Rex thought they hadn't a hope of finding out what had happened to Han but Polly was sure that there must be something they could do.

Once they were out of the woods and on the steep path down to the cove, everyone's mood seemed to lift. The wispy clouds parted and the moon shone through, silvering the calm water. Polly felt the tight feeling in her chest ease a little and she took a breath that seemed to go right down inside her.

"If the Green Lady didn't have anything to do with Han disappearing, could it have been the smugglers instead?" Polly wondered out loud. "What if he kept on following them?"

"No!" Li-Mei stepped back from Polly, shocked. "Robert and Nicholas were thoughtless, yes, but they wouldn't hurt their sister's dog on purpose!"

Rex stood next to
Li-Mei, gazing out at the water.
"Are you sure?" he said. "They might not have
wanted to, of course. But what if Han was
barking and they knew there were officers
of the Land Guard about?" He looked over
at Polly, crouching on Li-Mei's other side.
"The Land Guard were the force who tried to
prevent the smugglers. They rode up and down
the coast on horseback, trying to track down
the smuggled goods."

Li-Mei sniffed. "They never found anything.
A pack of fools, Sarah's father called them.

The Riding Officer walked into the church once, in the middle of a funeral service, saying that he was sure there was a cargo of French brandy hidden in there somewhere."

"In the church?" Polly stared at her.

"Yes. Stupid man. He searched all around the church, with the family cursing at him, and after all that the brandy was actually hidden in the grave, and they put the coffin in on top of it and dug it up the next week when he'd given up his search."

"Is that another of Nicholas's stories?" Polly asked doubtfully.

"No, no, I promise you, that one is true," Li-Mei assured her. "All the servants were talking about it. What Sarah was never sure about was whether or not the vicar knew…" She looked up at Rex and sighed. "I suppose you are right. If they thought that Han would get them discovered – I hate to think it but perhaps they did want to silence him."

"What did they do with the cargoes, besides putting them in graves?" Polly asked. "If they brought boats ashore here, surely they didn't bring the brandy and things up to the house, did they? People would have noticed a line of men with barrels and boxes of, um…"

"Tobacco," Rex put in. "That used to get smuggled, too. As did all sorts of things – French wines and silks and laces."

"That path is the only way out of the cove and it leads into the gardens," Polly said thoughtfully. "The family and the servants might have seen them, even if they were staying inside because of the Green Lady story."

"I am sure they did use this cove." Li-Mei walked a few steps along the damp sand, staring out at the sea. "We saw boats, once. Sarah was certain…"

Rex turned round, examining the cliffs. "Soft stone, this," he murmured. "There are caves, further up the coast. The cliffs are honeycombed with them."

"So there could be one here," Polly said. "Or maybe even a passage!" she added, her voice squeaking with excitement. "A secret passage!"

"Except there isn't," Li-Mei pointed out crossly. "Look – you can see that there isn't a cave. The cliff walls are sheer."

Polly bit her lip. "It could be behind the piles of rocks."

"But Sarah and I looked all along the cliffs when we were searching for Han. There's nothing there. No cave."

"She's right, you know."

Polly spun round, practically dropping her

torch as she found herself face to face with
William and Magnus. "Where did you two
come from?" she snapped.
"You nearly scared the
life out of me."

William smirked
at her. "I'm a ghost,
Polly, I can appear
where I like. And I get
to bring Magnus along, too.
What are you all doing, staring at the cliff and
looking for caves? You might have told us you
were going out. Magnus heard you gabbing
in the woods. The nearest cave's a mile or so
up the coast, at Merrymaid cove. We could go
exploring there, if you like." William sounded
rather hopeful and Magnus wagged his shaggy
grey tail.

"No, we were hoping there'd be a cave here,"

Polly said, lifting her torch and trailing the light along the cliff face. "We were trying to find out what might have happened to Han – Li-Mei's brother. We wondered if the smugglers might have…" she trailed off. "Then we started thinking, how did they bring their stuff out of the cove?" She moved the beam over the rocks again, then paused and looked back at Li-Mei. "When you and Sarah went searching, did you ever look behind the waterfall?"

"Behind it?" Rex snorted doubtfully. "There's nothing behind it. We'd see."

Polly shook her head. "I'm not sure. It's been a really hot summer so far and it's hardly rained at all but the stream that feeds the waterfall hasn't dried up. That's a lot of water, and it's all foaming and splashing. There could be something behind that curtain of water – it would only have to be a narrow crack in the rock face, not like a big cave mouth."

Li-Mei took a couple of paces forwards, staring at the waterfall. "Polly could be right," she admitted. "Sarah and I never looked behind all that water but what if there is a cave back there? It would be the perfect place for smugglers to hide their goods." Then she shivered a little. "It looks cold."

"And slippery," Polly agreed. "But this could be the answer to what happened to Han. Come on." She looked round at them all. Even Rex didn't seem particularly enthusiastic.

"Couldn't we wait until tomorrow?" he growled sheepishly. "It's dark…"

"It's a cave," Polly pointed out. "It'll be dark in the daytime, too, won't it?"

"I suppose so." Rex stared gloomily down at his feet. "Damp makes my paws ache."

Polly rolled her eyes. Rex was perfectly happy to go dancing about in the sea. She wasn't quite sure why the possibility of a tunnel was making them all so feeble. To her it sounded like something out of the best sort of adventure books. She felt like she ought to have a bottle of ginger beer with her. Polly huddled her hoodie closer round her neck and marched across the beach to the waterfall with the string of reluctant ghosts behind her.

The first night she had met Rex, they had jumped in and out of the spray of the waterfall, laughing and chasing each other, and it had been so much fun. Somehow, the thought of having to go through it made the water look a lot wetter. Polly hopped across the silvery stream that trickled over the beach and out towards the sea, soaking away into the sand as it went, and pressed herself up against the cliff face, trying to peer sideways behind the cascade of water. It was impossible to see anything, even with the torch. Flinching, she pulled up her sleeve and stuck her hand into the icy water with a tiny yelp.

"Can you feel anything?" Li-Mei demanded. The little dog was standing on Polly's trainers, twitching every time the water splashed her.

"No… Just solid rock. I think we need to go higher up." The waterfall bounced off a series of big rocks before it splashed down on to the beach – they would make it even harder to spot a cave opening, Polly thought.

Rex managed to leap up on top of the rocks in one easy bound. "What are you all waiting for?" he called down.

"William, can you help me?" Polly put her torch between her teeth, and with William shoving her up and Rex pulling on her sleeve, she struggled on to the slippery little ledge. It reminded her horribly of Li-Mei's story of the drowning girl.

William lifted Li-Mei up next to her and then he and Magnus scrambled up, too. "I think there is a darker patch," he said, "between this rock and that one right under the water. It could be an opening."

"Right under the water. It would be."
Magnus sighed. "I hate getting wet." He
looked sideways at Polly as if to say this was all
her fault.

"All right." Polly gripped the torch tightly,
shut her eyes and stepped sideways along the
rock, reaching out blindly with her free hand.
The shock of the cold waterfall made her gasp,
and she gulped water and choked, feeling her
feet slip on the mossy rock. Panicking, she
tried to grab at the rock wall – but there was
nothing there, only emptiness. "It's here," she
spluttered. "Be careful, it's so slippery!"

She felt Rex's great bulk come past her,
pushing her gently into the dark space and
out of the water, and then they were standing
there, the pair of them, gazing around at a
dark tunnel, lit by the faint beam of Polly's
torch.

Li-Mei erupted through the curtain of water, shaking herself into a damp little puffball. "You were right!" she said, and Polly decided to ignore how surprised she sounded. "Oh… If only I could show Sarah. She would be so excited."

"Are we going further in, then?" Magnus asked gloomily. "I can still just about see with the moonlight but it'll get darker if we go on. And colder."

Li-Mei snorted. "You can stay here if you're

afraid. *I* am going on."

"He isn't afraid," William said quickly. "He just likes being dismal. Come on, Magnus, this is an adventure. I wonder where it goes?"

"Under the house, perhaps," Rex said, questing forwards. "Into the cellars? Well, Li-Mei, are you coming?"

After her brave words, the Pekingese had stopped and was gazing anxiously into the darkness ahead.

She looked over at Rex and scratched at the damp rock of the floor. "We might find him," she said huskily. "I've wanted to know what happened all these years. What if we do find him? His bones…"

Polly swallowed hard. "Then we'll take them back with us," she whispered, crouching down to put her arms around the little dog. "We'll bury him in that little patch next to the Chinese garden. I bet we can make a headstone for him out of something."

"Yes." Li-Mei shook her ears determinedly. "Yes, I suppose."

They set off, Polly holding on to Rex's collar with one hand and the torch with the other, shining it around the tunnel. It was hard to tell whether it was natural or whether the smugglers had dug it out of the cliff themselves. After a few metres, though, Polly was almost sure she could see tool marks in the rocky walls. She couldn't imagine how long it must have taken to dig.

"I think it was a smaller cave and then it was opened up," Rex said, sniffing at the walls. "The smugglers must have tunnelled through."

"I suppose so," William agreed. "The tunnel must come out in the gardens somewhere. No wonder they wanted everyone tucked up inside, scared of the Green Lady."

"Oh!" Polly squeaked as her foot skidded on a loose shard of rock.

"Be careful!" Rex caught her sleeve in his teeth. "Slow down!"

"What is it?" Polly asked sharply, as her torch shimmered over a pile of rocks in front of them. "Oh, we can't get through."

"A rockfall." Rex edged closer. "The ceiling's collapsed and we don't know when

it happened. There could be more to fall."
He ducked back as a shower of stones came
bouncing down the pile. "See?"

"Yes…" Polly said, but she was still creeping
closer. She had seen something, gleaming in the
torchlight – a kingfisher flash of shining blue.

"Polly, be careful!" Rex hissed. "It could all
come down on top of you!"

"I don't think it will. This fell a
long time ago, Rex. Look." She
reached in and picked out
a piece of the shining blue
and shone the torch on it
for the others to see – it was
porcelain, the colour still rich
even under the rock dust.

"My statue!" Li-Mei yelped.

"No. The other statue. It has to be,
doesn't it? You said that it had disappeared."

Li-Mei crept closer. "Yes. Soon after Han did. Sarah's mama thought one of the maids had broken it and didn't want to say. She was so cross…" She whimpered. "It reminds me so much of Han."

"What was that?" Magnus shifted suddenly and Polly saw the fur rise on the back of his neck.

"I heard it, too." Rex took Polly's sleeve in his teeth again, pulling her away from the rockfall. Polly stumbled back, still clutching the piece of blue china.

"It isn't the rocks," she gasped. "It's coming from behind us."

Magnus made a low growl. "We'll be trapped if the ceiling falls in. We need to get you out of here."

Polly swallowed, realizing that she was probably the only one actually in danger. But then Li-Mei began to whine, over and over, all the while staring wide-eyed at the cave entrance and the waterfall beyond.

"Look…" Polly lifted the torch and traced it over the water and, at the same time, the noises seemed to sharpen and it was clear what they were.

Footsteps.

Five or six shadowy figures were shuffling towards them, laden down with barrels and boxes, muttering in low voices. They were dressed in breeches and loose jackets, with scarves muffled round their faces.

"What is it?" Polly whispered in a strangled voice. The passageway seemed colder than ever and she was reminded of the strange vision of the Green Lady that Li-Mei had shown her. Her insides felt cold and wobbly in just the same way.

"The smugglers," Rex murmured. "It has to be. I don't think they can see us, Polly, don't be afraid. They … they come with the place. I think."

Polly and William and the dogs pressed themselves back against the wall of the tunnel, and let the ghosts march past. To Polly's relief, none of the men looked sideways at all – it was as if they were still in their own time, completely separate from their watchers. They carried on up to the rockfall and then seemed to melt through it as if it wasn't there. Clearly, in their day, it hadn't been.

"What happened to them?" Polly whispered as the last eerie figure disappeared. "Why are they ghosts? Did they die here?" She looked up at the ceiling of the tunnel anxiously.

"No… They were only part of the story." Li-Mei was still peering back at the entrance under the waterfall, a few metres behind them. "Look. Oh, Han…"

A tiny form had broken through the water and was stomping determinedly forwards, shaking the drops out of his ears as he came.

"Han…" Li-Mei whimpered, as he hurried past her. "Han, look out!"

It was almost as if the little dog heard her. He looked around anxiously and then up, as dust and tiny pieces of stone began to shower down on top of him – and then the ceiling of the tunnel collapsed, burying him under a pile of broken stone.

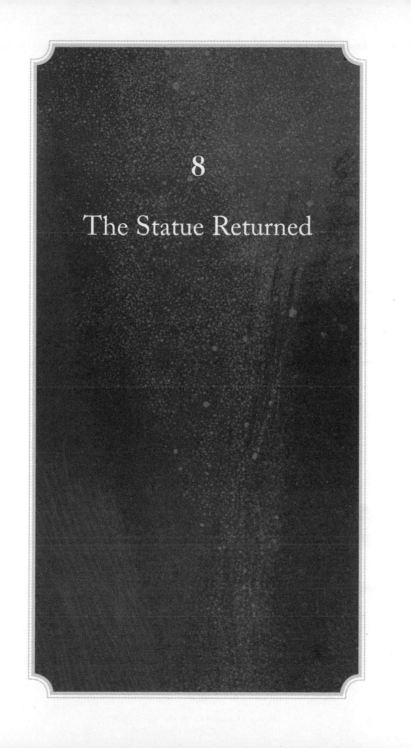

8

The Statue Returned

"Han!" Li-Mei darted forwards, scrabbling at the pile of rock and letting out a long, full-throated howl.

Polly dashed after the little dog and scooped her up. "It's not now, Li-Mei, it's not real. It all happened a long time ago."

"It's still happening." William pulled Polly back. "Li-Mei, look. Someone else is coming."

Polly huddled against the wall with Li-Mei in her arms and they watched as one more figure came creeping through the tunnel. He was smaller than the others and Polly thought the clothes he was wearing looked grander – there was a frill at the collar of the boy's shirt and his jacket was made of a finer fabric than the men's rough coats. "Nicholas?" she whispered to Li-Mei. "Or Robert?"

"Nicholas," Li-Mei growled back, snapping her teeth. "Little beast." And then, "Look what he's carrying!"

"The statue!" Polly peered closer as the boy came past them. "Yes, it is. Oh, Li-Mei. This isn't the same night. It can't be. I think he must have worked out what happened to Han."

They watched as Nicholas crouched down by the pile of fallen rock and found a flat place to stand the statue on. He lifted the blue porcelain Fu Dog into place and hung his head.

"Sorry, Han," they heard him whisper, his voice floating towards them with the dust.

"You shouldn't have followed us. You should have stayed safe with Sarah. Thank God she didn't go after you. I wish I could take you up to the house and bury you properly and stop Sarah searching for you, but I can't move all this. The boys aren't going to clear it, they say they'll find another place to land the cargo. Now the tunnel's started to collapse, they reckon it's not safe down here. You'll have to stay under there, little dog."

They watched as he stroked the china figure and then turned to plod miserably back along the tunnel to the waterfall. As he vanished through the curtain of water, another shower of stones came tumbling down and the blue porcelain lion shattered into pieces.

Polly shuddered. "Is that why Han never came back … as a ghost, I mean?" she whispered. "Because the statue broke?"

"I suppose so," Rex agreed. "People see the rest of us – children climb over my statue and everyone admires Li-Mei's lion figure on the mantelpiece. We need that – we need love, I suppose. Han was buried here under the rocks, out of sight, and so was this figure."

Polly stood up, pulling away from Rex and the others. If only she could find all the pieces… She dropped to her knees beside the pile of rock, carefully levering out the shards of blue.

There was a scrabbling behind her, and Li-Mei appeared and started to dig gently at the pile, burrowing with her paws and then pulling out the pieces of china with her teeth. "Do you think this will make any difference?" she asked Polly, spitting out a mouthful of rock dust.

"It's got to be worth a try. Let me help, it's easier with fingers." Polly leaned forwards and started to sift carefully through the rocks. After a minute or two, she took off her hoodie to pile the pieces on, so they could carry them back.

"I don't like this," Rex growled, clawing out a piece of blue china. "It feels to me like the rest of the ceiling could go at any minute."

"I wonder what happens to ghosts – or whatever we are – when they get crushed under tons of falling rock," Magnus muttered.

"We must be nearly done," Polly said. "I can't see any more pieces. Oh, except there, look."

She reached out for one last fragment of blue…

"It's going!" William screamed and Polly looked up. Everything seemed to have slowed – there was more dust in the air and a dreadful pattering as tiny pieces of rock shuddered down from the ceiling.

Rex let out a roar. "Polly, move!" he cried and barged into her, hurling her across the passage. She flew sideways, huddling her arms up around her head as the roof of the tunnel beyond her collapsed with a sliding, thundering smash.

Polly lay there for a moment, half stunned, her ears ringing. She wasn't sure what was happening. All the air seemed to have been knocked out of her. She dragged herself up against the wall. Her hand was so tightly clenched round the tiny fragment of porcelain that she could feel it cutting into her hand.

"Polly! Polly? Are you all right?" Rex was nosing at her frantically. "Talk to me!"

William leaned down to help her up. "Another great chunk of the roof came down," he told her in a shaky voice.

"Where's Li-Mei?" she gasped.

"Here…" The Pekinese shuffled forwards from her place pressed against the rock wall. Her voice was muffled by the sleeve of Polly's hoodie, clutched in her teeth. The bedraggled hoodie trailed along behind her, with the china fragments still piled on top.

"You rescued the pieces!"

"I wasn't going to leave him behind again,"
Li-Mei said. "Please can we get out of here?"

"What are we going to do with all this?"
Polly asked, looking at her hoodie spread out
on the floor of the Red Drawing Room. The
china fragments seemed so sad – dull and
broken and dusty. Some of the pieces were
quite large and Polly could even see what
the bigger pieces had been – one painted eye
peered up at her mournfully. She had tried
putting them back together, like a jigsaw,
but it was just too complicated. Especially as
she was enough her mother's daughter not
to want to use glue. The statue was worth
hundreds of pounds, maybe even thousands
– or it would have been if it wasn't in bits.

Sticking it together badly would just make everything worse. "I suppose I could give it to Mum, and she could try and get it mended," Polly mused. "But where would I say I'd found it? And I expect she'd have to send it away to a restorer. We want it to stay here, that's the whole point."

"Perhaps we don't need to stick it back together at all," Rex murmured. "Just being here, with Li-Mei's statue and the portrait, that should help."

"I can't leave it in the middle of the floor," Polly pointed out. "We have to hide it somewhere."

"Up the chimney?" Magnus suggested. He stood in the fireplace, next to the grate, and stuck his head up the chimney. "There's often a little shelf in the side of the wall – makes a good hiding place— Ooof!" He backed out again, his face darkened with greasy, sooty smuts.

"Maybe not," William sniggered, and Magnus stalked out of the room.

"You could put them in the cabinet," Li-Mei suggested, walking over to the red lacquer cabinet underneath Sarah's portrait.

But Polly shook her head. "No, that's no good. Sometimes the volunteers open it, to show off the mother-of-pearl inlay on the inside."

Li-Mei snorted. "So? They don't open the secret compartment, do they? Sarah's father showed it to her. It was their secret. He used to put peppermint drops in it for her. Unlatch the doors, Polly."

Polly opened the little gold hook and the doors swung open, the iridescent mother-of-pearl patterns glimmering in the torchlight.

"Lift me up," Li-Mei said. "Yes, now where is it…? Here! Open this drawer. And now this one. You see, you can only find the secret space when they are both open. There is a little catch, feel there at the back of that top drawer."

Polly brushed her fingers along the wood and felt her nail hook round a tiny catch. She pulled at it nervously, hoping she wasn't about to damage a priceless antique.

"Pull the drawer right out," Li-Mei told her impatiently. "Come on. There, you see."

Polly nodded. At the back of the two drawers was a hidey hole – you would only realize it was there if you took out the drawers and measured them against the side of the cabinet. Pulling the catch had opened a false back and now the secret compartment was open.

"Put the pieces inside there," Li-Mei ordered

her. "Then they'll be under Sarah's portrait. The statue will be back in her favourite Chinese room, where it's supposed to be. And then…" She sighed. "Then I don't know."

"Then we watch and you think of your brother," Rex told her gently. "Magnus. Come back, old friend. We need you."

Magnus slunk back into the room so quickly that Polly thought he had probably been lurking outside the door. He was sootless now but he was still cross that William had laughed at him.

"What?" he growled. "Got things to do."

Rex nudged him with his nose. "We need to watch for the little dog. A vigil. Someone needs to show that he is missed."

Magnus sighed and slumped down in front of the cabinet, watching as Polly reset the catch and gently pushed the drawers back in. He laid his long nose on his paws and huffed as Li-Mei came to sit beside him. "Couldn't we have a vigil with cushions?" he muttered to her, but she ignored him, sitting up very straight and staring at the cabinet.

Polly and William came to sit beside them, and Rex, too, so that they were a semicircle in front of the cabinet and the portrait, watching the faint gleam of the lacquer in the moonlight. Polly put on her hoodie and set her torch down on her lap. Now she could just see the pinkish-brown of Sarah's dress and the shape of Han behind her.

She blinked, feeling suddenly sleepy now that she was sitting down and thinking that she agreed with Magnus, cushions would be nice. Did she need to think sad thoughts again? she wondered vaguely. She was just so tired, thinking was hard… One of the dogs nudged against her hand and she jerked awake again, whispering, "Sorry."

"Not to worry," the dog murmured back. "Not at all. What are you doing?"

Polly swallowed, turning her head to see a little dark-eyed dog. "I think we're waiting for you."

It was almost growing light by the time they had explained to Han what had happened. For him, it seemed only a short while since that terrifying moment when he had been caught in the rockfall.

Li-Mei was sitting next to her brother, half the time nosing at him lovingly and the other half telling him what a fool he had been to go rushing after the smugglers without her and Sarah.

"At least I didn't get taken in by that stupid ghost!" he pointed out. "I could smell that it was young Davy Trellan in a dress as soon as he got close! What's happened to your nose, Li-Mei?"

"Davy Trellan? It was not!"

"Most certainly was. Smelled of fish."

"Half the village smelled of fish!" Li-Mei yapped.

"Well, maybe. Ghosts don't, though, do they?" Han put his head on one side, examining his sister with the same bright bulging eyes.

"But how did they make him glow?" Polly asked. "Li-Mei showed me what happened that night – I could see the greenish light, coming towards us. It wasn't natural."

Han shook his head. "Some sort of luminous paint, I suppose. It was all over him, in streaks. A clever trick."

"I didn't even know people made luminous paint then," Polly said, surprised.

"Robert was always reading strange journals about chemicals and experiments," Li-Mei said. "It's the kind of thing he would have loved."

Han nodded. "So, what happened to the statue? The one that Nicholas put on top of the rockfall?"

"It broke," Li-Mei told him sadly. "More of the rocks fell on it. You can see the pieces, we brought them back and put them in the secret compartment. Polly, will you open it again?"

William held the torch as Polly unlatched the cabinet and slid out the drawers, trying hard to remember where the catch was. The false back sprang open and her breath stilled in her throat. Staring haughtily back at her was the statue, no longer in pieces, but the twin of Li-Mei's, perfectly whole.

"Lift it out," Li-Mei yelped. "Put it on the mantelpiece with mine!" She was dancing around Polly's feet so frantically that Rex leaned down and caught her by the scruff of her neck to hold her still.

"Stop it, do you want to trip her up and smash it again?"

Polly cradled the statue against her torn

hoodie, stroking the
china whiskers, and
then lifted it gently
on to the opposite
end of the
mantelpiece from
its twin. Then she
stepped back to
admire them both. The

two Pekingese leaped up on to one of the sofas
to look, too. Han was balanced dangerously on
the arm of the sofa, Polly noticed. He didn't
seem to have got any more careful.

"What am I going to say to Mum?" Polly
sighed.

"You think people will notice, then?" Rex
asked.

"Of course they will! For a start, the room
description says that there's only one statue!

And Mum loves this room – she's been working on this part of the family history, trying to find out more about Lawrence Penhallow."

"Well, perhaps you could tell her you found it," Rex said.

"In the secret compartment," Li-Mei agreed. "It's even true. You could say that you opened it and accidentally found the secret part."

"Maybe… I'm not supposed to touch the furniture, not anything delicate." Polly smiled at the little dog. "But she's going to be over the moon that we've found the statue and they're a pair again – and just in time for her special exhibition. Perhaps she'll just be so happy to have it back that she won't ask too many questions. And I bet she'll be excited about the secret compartment as well. I wish we could tell her about Lawrence Penhallow putting sweets in it for Sarah." Polly smiled to herself, remembering how strange it had felt to be someone else – almost. Sarah had been so brave, so determined, the way she'd refused to let the boys leave her behind. Maybe a little bit of that bravery had rubbed off on Polly? She hoped so… Somehow, a new school didn't seem quite as scary as it had before. Not compared to ghosts and smugglers and poor Li-Mei grieving for her brother all this time.

Polly ran her hand over Li-Mei's head and then Han's. "You know, you might not like this but you do actually look like lions. It's the way your fur sticks out, like a little mane. Fierce brave lion dogs."

"Exactly," Li-Mei said, puffing herself up, and Han gave a tiny growly roar.

Magnus sighed and leaned his muzzle on the sofa arm next to Han. "Wonderful. One of those creatures was bad enough. Do you have to encourage them?"

Rex licked Polly's ear and whispered, "You did very well to help Li-Mei find him, Polly. But you're my special person, remember."

Polly rubbed her cheek against his ear and murmured back. "Don't worry. I know. Always."

PENHALLOW HALL

TREASURES OF CHINA

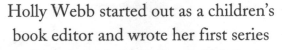

Holly Webb started out as a children's
book editor and wrote her first series
for the publisher she worked for.
She has been writing ever since, with
over one hundred books to her name.
Holly lives in Berkshire, with her
husband and three young sons. Holly's
pet cats are always nosying around
when she is trying to type on her laptop.

~

For more information
about Holly Webb visit
www.holly-webb.com